THE GRINGO MANIAC
MURDER SPREE

Published by Lisa Hagan Books 2015

Powered by

**SHADOW
TEAMS**

THE GRINGO MANIAC MURDER SPREE

JOSHUA P. WARREN

Contents

1

Damn, That's A Good Pina Colada

I could feel someone looking at me. I hate that feeling; especially since I'm running from the fucking law. I glanced down the bar, and there he sat—first time I ever saw him. Sure enough, he was staring at me. I'm a gringo, too, but this guy was white as a ghost, his head cocked with a straw fedora, beady eyes behind dark sunglasses, and a big, wide shit-eating grin on his face. His teeth were so white and perfect they looked weird. Maybe in his 50s, he appeared like a tourist, and yet perfectly at home.

"Hola amigo," sailed from his lips like a seagull. He seemed SO comfortable.

"Hola," I said, waiting to see if he was some kind of bounty hunter.

I've been all over place. Personally I think its bullshit that you can go to prison for selling a WEED. I think I can even argue that it's unconstitutional. But nobody seems to care what I think. As far as I can tell, the law is what a judge says the law is. And that's THAT. Especially in Tennessee. That's where I'm from. My name is Bill Wade. I'm 30 now. My friends used to call me Wild Bill Wade. That's because I've always really only been good at one thing, and that's kicking ass. Some guys have a talent for playing the piano, or throwing a ball, or painting a picture. Not me. For me, it's always just been one thing. I am excellent at kicking ass. And yes, it came in handy when I finally said "screw the States" and hopped a boat to Puerto Rico. The laws in Puerto Rico are strange.

That day was hot as hell, and all I wanted was a pina colada from the Barrachina in San Juan. They supposedly invented it there. Salsa music was bumping, parrots were squawking, the fountain was bubbling, the warm breeze was blowing, and there was a tall, white frosty drink in front of me, topped with a bright red cherry. I was almost relaxed, and now this . . .

I glanced down to see if he had a gun or badge on his side. Nope; only white shorts and white tennis shoes. I remember he was wearing a puffy, blue long-sleeved shirt, with the sleeves rolled up. I'm more of a plain t-shirt and surfer shorts guy with sandals.

"Salud," he said, raising his own pina colada. He sounded white as hell, and looked happy as a clam. We bumped glasses and I looked away. I could hear him suck deeply through his straw. Then I just knew he was gonna speak to me again. Yep . . .

"Damn, that's a good pina colada! Are you on vacation, amigo?" he said. His voice was almost graceful.

"Uh, I'm staying here for a while. I'm looking for some work."

"Oh," he perked up. "What brought you to the island?"

I inhaled and fumbled with my cell phone a bit. This was 2010, and wi-fi was sketchy.

"You know," I gave my standard answer, "I just needed one more trip to the beach, and this time I decided to stay for a while."

He chuckled and nodded. "I'm Dick Peck," he said, extending a hand.

As I shook it, he already had a business card in his left hand. I looked at the card. It was pretty simple; just a white card with black text:

Richard Peck III
Photographer
P.O. Box 16801
Asheville, NC 28816

I always hated calling guys "Dick."

"Nice to meet ya, Peck," I said. "I'm Bill." I looked him real straight in the eye. I'm a pretty big guy with black hair, and I thought I might intimidate him into shutting the fuck up. No go. He just kept grinning in some phony-ass way.

"I'm here to take pictures professionally," he said. "But I can't find my way around. I've been lost since I left the airport. I need a guide."

"Who are you taking pictures for?" I asked.

"National Geographic," he replied, then slurped through his straw again. "What do you do, amigo?"

"Ummm . . . I've been doing a lot of yard work."

"Just here?"

"All around the island," I said. "Wherever I can make a buck," I smiled.

"Where are you from?" he furrowed his brow.

"I'm from Tennessee."

"Oh SWEET, brother!" he exclaimed, extending his hand once again. "I'm from North Carolina."

We shook again briskly. That's when I first noticed the ring on his right hand. It was the only ring he wore. It was gold with a black face, emblazoned with the square and compasses. My grandfather wore one of those. I never understood exactly what those guys were about.

"So you know your way all around here?" he leaned closer, more relaxed. This guy was obviously trying to become my buddy now.

"Yeah, pretty much," I kept screwing around with my phone.

"It's a good day here. I'll pay you $100 to get me to the El Yunque," he said.

Screech! Hold the presses. $100? El Yunque rain forest was maybe an hour down the road—almost a straight shot. I sorta wanted to tell him I couldn't take advantage of him, and just show him some stuff on a map. But I was broke as a fuck-stick. I'd been bouncing from hostel to hostel, and $100 could get me five nights.

"You have a car?" I inquired.

"Oh yeah."

"Okay, I can take you there for $100."

"All right," he bellowed. "Muchas gracias, amigo!" He extended his hand again with another crazy grin. His teeth were almost too big for his mouth. I shook heartily and pulled a little closer. I guess we were gonna be friends now.

"When do you wanna leave?" I asked.

"Right now, when I finish this drink," he replied.

"And when do you wanna come back?"

"Oh . . .," he looked up in the air, "maybe 9 o'clock."

It was 1pm. That was $12.50 an hour for nothin'. I was definitely IN.

Ten minutes later, we were ambling over rocky, uneven, cobblestone, splashing through the occasional wet and stinky puddle. He rambled on about how pretty the island was, and various touristy bullshit, then we finally arrived at his black Nissan. Convertible. Jackpot! I hopped inside, and he sank behind the wheel, drawing the neck strap on his hat up to his jutting chin. He kind of looked like an old lady this way. The words coming from his mouth were like the "nah, nah, nah, nah, nah," that teachers spoke in the Charlie Brown cartoons. Wish I'd listened. Then again, if I had, I might have ended it right then and there. But I didn't. And now I have a fucking novel. Here's what happened next . . .

* * *

Reggaton played on the stereo, and I couldn't help but bob along. I closed my eyes. The warm wind whipped through my hair. Pieces of sunlight glinted and glanced on my eyelids, breaking through each fiber of the huge leaves overhead. Peck kept talking about f-stops and exposures and how much he liked to shoot on both film and digital. I just tuned him out and relaxed.

"Nah, nah, nah?" . . . "Nah, nah, nah, Bill?"

"Huh?" I jerked up.

"Right or left, amigo? Right or left!"

"Oh! Uh . . . right," I said. Guess I had to pay attention now.

He swung right and about whipped my head off. I sat up, eyes wide open, and realized I needed to earn my keep. But, as it turns out, that was the last time he even needed my advice.

"Why did you come here, amigo?" he asked, eyes trained on the road.

Fuck it. "Ok," I said, "I was arrested in Johnson City for selling weed. About five times. And now I'm facing prison time, so I ran. I came here, to get outta the states."

Peck was quiet for a bit, then he shook his head in a very understanding way. "Ok," he said. While looking straight ahead, he twisted his body to the right, and reached back for his black backpack, digging around in a pocket. A couple moments later, he pulled out a little joint.

"Cool amigo," he grinned. "Wanna smoke this?"

I laughed and held up my hand. "Ah, no thanks. I just sold it. I'm not a big smoker."

"Ok," he said. "But now you've got me craving some Mary Jane, amigo." He took both hands off the wheel, driving with his fucking knees, and magically produced a lighter from nowhere. It was a torch light, but even its blue flame struggled as he blew down the highway at 60 mph. I couldn't believe this crazy bastard was smoking a joint while driving. I'd only known him maybe 30 minutes.

"What's your story?" I screamed over the wind.

"I was an insurance salesman for thirty years," he yelled. "I had a wife and two kids. Once my kids were grown, I decided to pursue my dream of photography. So now I'm divorced, and I'm here!"

I nodded. "Okay. Cool."

Our car headed farther and farther up the winding road. Little by little, I glimpsed the ocean, a rich blue, down below, peeking through the lush, green vegetation, white froth crashing quietly on distant rocks. We were going higher and higher. Soon, we'd passed through the gates of the El Yunque, the only rainforest that is a U.S. National Park. That's when I first noticed the black SUV behind us.

My spidey-senses tingled. "I think we may have some cops on us," I said.

"Huh?" Peck looked into the rear-view mirror. The SUV was like a dark, sleek predator.

"Might wanna ditch the joint," I suggested.

He groaned. "GOD DAMMNIT!" he shouted, tossing the joint into the wind. It literally blew back and bounced off the SUV windshield.

"Aw shit!" I exclaimed. "You should have swallowed it!"

It was clear that Peck had lost it for a moment, but now his composure was back instantly.

"Just hold tight, amigo. Let's see if they keep up with us."

I was holding my breath, waiting to see blue lights at any moment.

"Hey amigo," Peck said calmly. "Are you good at fighting?"

I snickered. "Yes, actually, I am."

"I don't like to fight." He sounded reflective.

"Yeah, well . . . just follow the speed limit," I replied helpfully.

As we ascended the mountains, the giant trees drooped over us. The exotic land transformed into a green-gray throat, swallowing us deeper. Mist set in and waterfalls cascaded by the lane. The ancient natives here, the Taino Indians, believed God lived at the top of this mountain, hidden in the clouds. "Are those cops?" I wondered. Squeezed between cliffs and waterfalls, we were trapped on this road.

There was a slight, dirt pull-off on the right side of the road, near a bend. "I'm gonna pull over and let them by," Peck resolved. He eased off the pavement and onto the moist ground. My stomach sank when the SUV crept in behind us. Peck took a deep breath and sighed. Now we were both silent. It crossed my mind to run.

The doors opened slowly on the SUV. First, the driver stepped out. He was Puerto Rican—tall and scowling, wearing a black baseball cap. The passenger door opened, and a shorter, but similar man, came out. They walked slowly toward the car. I didn't see any badges or guns. Peck sat still, looking ahead, almost trance-like.

I imaged the men would split; one approaching each side of the car. Instead, they stuck together, both of them ambling up to Peck's side. The tall man said something in Spanish. His voice was firm.

"Hola amigo," Peck smiled. "No hablo espanol," he said sweetly.

The demeanor of the tall man changed quickly. He was even more assertive, repeating his Spanish phrase more aggressively.

"I don't understand you, hombre," Peck replied matter-of-factly.

Things felt so tense, I didn't even want to look over at the interaction.

At that point, the tall man lowered his face to Peck's and his hand moved to his side. He was in gunslinger mode, though I still had not actually seen a pistol. The shorter man's right hand took the same position on his body. The tall man shouted Spanish again, right into Peck's face. It was as if he believed this gringo could indeed speak Espanol.

Peck shook his head, paused for a moment, then looked the tall man right in the eye. I couldn't believe what he said next: "You need to chill the fuck out, amigo."

"Huh?"

Peck remained calm. "You. Need. To. Chill-the-fuck-out. Amigo."

The tall man glanced at the short man, then drew out a radio.

"No FUCKING hablo!" Peck screamed.

The next few moments were a blur. I saw a glint of sunlight, then my ears were shattered. "POW, POW, POW, POW, POW, POW, POW, POW."

Peck was shooting the FUCK out of these guys. My stomach dropped in the most sickening way.

Then there was silence. I fumbled for words.

"Oh shit! Oh shit!" I exclaimed.

"It's all cool, amigo," he said. It seemed like a dream. I feared him, and he could see it.

The men he shot were gone. I had scrambled back over my seat, confused and unsettled.

"Calm DOWN, amigo," he said. "It's no biggie."

"Oh shit!" I exclaimed again. I jumped out of the car, head spinning, scanning frantically to see if anyone else was around.

"Where the hell are you going amigo?"

"I…I don't know," I said. I was so confused.

"Look," he leaned over, "everything is cool, amigo. Just chill the fuck out."

Those were some of the last words he had said to them, so I took full notice.

"Seriously amigo," he said. "Chill the fuck out and help me."

"Help you what?"

"We're stuck here amigo," he said. "We gotta get this car outta the way so we can get the fuck outta here."

"I'm not part of this!" I screamed louder than anything I've ever said in my life.

"Dude!" Peck screamed. "I know exactly WHO YOU ARE. Now help me!"

I couldn't process his words. "What?"

He closed his eyes and squinted them. "Amigo . . . we have to get the fuck outta here. Listen to me."

Next thing I remember, he was outta the car and digging in the pocket of the tall man (now dead as hell). In moments, he had fished out the SUV key.

"Here," he tossed it to me. "Back it up so we can get outta here."

I don't know why I followed his orders. But where the hell else was I gonna go and what the hell else was I gonna do? I don't remember exactly what happened, but I backed up the SUV and the next thing I recall we were on the rainforest road again. I was stunned—I guess in shock— when I looked back over to him and realized I was now a victim—a hostage—in the car with a maniac. For a long time, as we sped through the winding turns, I was afraid to speak. Finally . . .

"What the fuck just happened?" I asked.

"What do you mean?"

"I thought you didn't like to fight."

"Fighting? No." he said. "Shooting, yes."

I felt like I was gonna throw up. "I want out," I said.

"Too late for that, amigo," he actually chuckled, throwing his head back. It looked like the wind would blow his straw hat away, even with the chin strap.

"NO. I want out!" I exclaimed.

He flashed his weird, white grin. "I've GOT YOU now motherfucker!" he laughed like a madman.

"Stop the fucking car now!" I demanded.

"Fine," he said flatly. "We're here now anyway."

It's funny how your memory flashes from point-to-point when something truly surprising happens. Next thing I recall was the two of us sitting on the edge of a gravel trail. The spooky canopy of the rainforest, its giant leaves and twisting roots, shined and hung all around us, and a swift stream rushed nearby. The white noise of a distant waterfall subtly masked our words.

Peck was now calm and fatherly. "I know you're running from the law," he said.

"Yeah, join the fucking club," I snapped sarcastically. That's not even what I meant to say. I meant to imply that he was now running from the law, as well. But I wasn't making sense. Nonetheless, he understood.

"Look, amigo," Peck sounded incredibly at ease, "those guys I just shot were not cops. They were drug dealers."

"What are you talking about? Drug dealers?"

"That's right," Peck nodded. "I had to kill them or they were gonna kill us. I'm not really a photographer. I'm . . . similar to a DEA officer."

"Are you going to arrest me?"

"No amigo. Not if you help me out. But you are on the list."

"What?"

"Yeah," he said. "I have a list of people who need to be brought to justice. And you're on it, amigo." He sighed sadly.

"To kill? That's not legal," I fumbled for words.

"It depends, amigo," he said. "That's why I'm in Puerto Rico. This is not a state. Once you come here, the laws are fucked up."

He was right. I had forgotten that.

"But law doesn't really matter anyway," he said. "I'm not exactly DEA. I'm with a more clandestine branch of the government."

"Oh, and what is that?" I asked defiantly.

"It doesn't really have a name," he mused. "It's just a bunch of numbers that no one can remember. Office number 5839274—some kind of bullshit like that. So we just call it 'Numbers.' Our job is to go to places where drug dealers can just be killed, I mean brought to justice, and bring them to justice. And sooner or later, many of them end up here in Puerto Rico. And when they get here, I just go out and well, sometimes have to shoot their ass. And the problemo is solved, amigo."

I stared at him for a moment. "And you're gonna kill me?"

"Nope," he said. "I'm not gonna kill you. I have an offer for you."

"Yeah?" I was listening.

"What's the worst you ever did, amigo?"

"I just sold weed; that was it."

"Well I tell you what," he leaned closer. "You help me out while I go bring some of these guys to justice, and I'll see that you get a full pardon. The running will be over. AND, AND," he raised a finger, "I'll pay you."

"You could get me pardoned from the law?" I was suspicious.

"Yes," he said confidently.

"Meaning they would no longer be looking for me? I would be a FREE man?"

"That's right amigo. A clean slate," he slapped his knee with finality.

"And why, exactly, would you offer this to me?" I inquired.

"Dude," he said, drawing back as if the next words from his mouth should be blaringly obvious, "you're from Tennessee, right? And they say you're definitely good at kicking ass."

I just looked at him a moment. Some guys have a naïve trust for those who come from the same neck of the woods. I nodded. He grinned again, and opened his arms in an accepting way. This did not add up.

"Tonight we're gonna go party in San Juan. All you

have to do is back me up while I track down some of this scum. Cool?"

* * *

Hours later it was dusk, and the two of us were sitting at a breezy outdoor patio on San Sebastian Street, the "party street" in Old San Juan. My fork picked bits of cold, zesty fish from a fresh glass of ceviche. My head was still swirling. Peck was kicking back with a glass of dark rum, smiling, watching the people move past on the narrow, blue bricks of the street.

I stared at him. My head had cleared some, and my suspicion built by the minute. "Do you have any ID?"

"What's that, amigo?"

"Do you have a badge or something to prove you're with the law?"

Peck's face morphed into that big weird smile.

"Why sure I do, amigo," he spoke gently.

Peck fished around in his front pocket for a minute. "Here ya go." He pulled out his hand shooting me a bird. I was exasperated, though he howled with laughter. "No, seriously, here." He reached into his back pocket and pulled out a little wallet. He opened it and held it up. There was a pic of his grinning ass with an eagle seal and a bunch of other official-looking bullshit on it.

"You wanna call the cops and check this?" he asked rhetorically. "And then they'll call me and say, 'You had to blow your cover? Who saw your ID?' And I'll say 'William Jones Wade, son of Clyde and Cathy Wade, born November 3, 1980, resident of 1353 West Laurel Avenue, Johnson City, social security number 294-66-9173.' And they'll say 'Good fucking job Agent Peck. You get another Christmas bonus.' And I'll pull out my gun and drag your ass right down to the San Juan office. You might be out of prison in ten years. What say ye?"

My stomach sank a little deeper.

I thought of running. "I need to go to the bathroom," I said.

"Man, don't be stupid," Peck stuffed the wallet back in his shorts. "If you try to run, you're screwed amigo. I already put a bug up your ass."

"What?"

"I already stuffed a bug way up your dirty, stinky, sweaty asshole, that's what."

Needless to say, I was confused. "What do you mean?"

Peck took a sip of rum and leaned closer. "You've heard of Roswell, right?"

"Yeah."

"Well when those aliens crashed we got all kinds of technology from them. Didn't you know that? Don't you watch the History Channel, amigo? I put a tracking device in your ass and you didn't even know it. That's what probing is all about. We're pros at it now. Your asshole is lighting up 15 satellite screens right now. We know, dude, we can track you like an animal now."

I shook my head. "I don't believe you."

"DUDE," Peck stressed, now pulling a pack of cigarettes from his pocket. "You don't believe in aliens man? They figured it out millions of years ago. They invented it. The ultimate device in the universe that tells you everything about any living organism. It's a work of sheer, cosmic genius. Only problem: it has to go up your ass. And now you've got one. Trust me."

"Why can't I just shit it out then?"

"You don't understand, amigo. It's there to stay, at least until I take it out." He kicked back and lit up his smoke with a cheap Bic. "Just relax. You help me and I'll help you."

"But . . . but why would you help me?" I stumbled.

"I told you, amigo, you're from Tennessee. And I need somebody like you to help me kick some ass down here. And maybe you can be a fall guy if shit hits the fan."

"Oh great."

"Just follow the rules. I do this all the time."

"What rules?" I exclaimed.

"Just do what I tell you. And tonight, that means you sleep in a nice cushy hotel in Old San Juan, because tomorrow night we're gonna work on something special."

"What's that?"

"I'll show you," he smiled. "Let's head down San Sebastian a little ways."

∗　∗　∗

Soon enough we were in another bar; a dingy, dim one with craploads of old advertisements and band promos half-hanging from the walls. There was a horny couple making out at the end of the bar, so I felt extra uncomfortable when Peck slid his chair as close to mine as possible. For the first time, I could clearly see some of the wrinkles on his face, and smell the sharp scent of his cigarette breath. It was dark outside, but he still wore his sunglasses.

"Look across the street," he rasped.

I glanced out the large open doorway, and there was another bar, similar to this one, bustling with an eclectic mix of people. It was called Oscuro.

"What? That bar?" I said.

"Yeah, dude. That's how we get to El Chupacabra."

"Chupacabra?" my brow twisted.

There was a laugh behind the bar. I looked up to see the large bartender, tan skin with a grey beard. He'd been about to ask if we wanted another round. I hadn't intended for him to hear me. Peck laughed along with the barkeep. "Yes sir!" Peck bellowed. "Chupacabra!"

"I know something about de chupacabra!" he bellowed with a deep voice. "My grandfather told me."

Peck perked up. "Oh? What's that?"

The barkeep began telling a story, despite the fact a couple other patrons down the ancient wooden bar were obviously ready for another round.

"My grandfather," he began, "lived up de mountain," he waved his hand. "And when he was a young man, de chickens and goats and cows were getting killed. All der blood drank. Dese were poor people, and so dis was a big deal. De men of de village got a large, metal box, a trap, and put a goat in it as bait. Dat night de dogs started barking. Den men gathered around with axes and rifles, and saw de door of de box had shut. It was rocking back and forth like something big was inside. Nobody wanted to be de first to open it. Finally, dey get courage to open de trap. Inside was de dead goat, drained of blood, and nothing else. De chupacabra had somehow escaped, like he was not of dis world."

Peck clapped his hands and laughed knowingly. "Exactly amigo! Exactly!"

"I thought they were just mangy coyotes," I added. The barkeep shook his head, as did Peck.

"These things are from another dimension," Peck said matter-of-factly.

"So you want another drink?" the barkeep asked.

"Si. Two more Don Qs for me and mi amigo," Peck said. The barkeep walked away to get the rum.

"So we're chasing an alien?" I said to Peck.

"No, no, no," Peck declared. "We're gonna find a very real motherfucker."

"Tonight?"

"Nah. Tomorrow we'll start. After this drink, let's get some rest."

Peck settled the tab when the rums arrived. "Ready to call it a night, amigo?" he asked.

"What about my money?" I said.

"Ahh, okay," Peck responded resolutely. He pulled out his wallet and counted out $200 in $20 bills. That was 100 more than I expected. "Let's go the hotel now. You have your own room."

"And tomorrow we find the chupacabra?" I inquired.

"You're goddamn right," he said. "You're goddamn right."

2

The Chupacabra

Nightmares haunted me, and in my sweaty tosses and turns, I'd gotten very little sleep. Around noon, I met Peck at Café Cultura for a cup of fine coffee and some sweet pastries. My entire soul was troubled. The sweeping Spanish beauty of the old city mocked me. Of course I wanted to run, but that's what I'd been doing for so long, and I was sick of it.

Peck relaxed across from me, wearing those black sunglasses again, propped back with his stupid white tennis shoes, and the whole day seemed unnatural. Everyone in the café was having a smashing time. Touristy women giggled like they were at Disney World, but I felt the weight of another world on my shoulders.

"So we're gonna find the chupacabra?" I asked.

"Oh fuck yeah," he replied.

"So we're looking for some kind of alien?"

"Oh, fuck no!" he exclaimed. "You don't know yet amigo."

I was frustrated. "Don't know what?"

Peck leaned forward, over the small, round table.

"We're not gonna get that chupacabra. We're gonna get the Chupacabra."

I was already fed up with his elusiveness. "Okay, and what is the chupacabra?"

Peck smiled. "All these drug dealers have code names. And the one who runs this region is El Chupacabra. I couldn't tell you last night."

"The chupacabra is a drug dealer?"

"It's a code name. All the kingpin bastards on this island use code names. And the big one around here is El Chupacabra."

"Oh, okay," I replied. "So we're not looking for an alien?"

Peck smiled and leaned back. "Not yet amigo. Not yet."

"So who is El Chupacabra?"

Peck strained toward me again. "Now this guy is ONE SICK FUCK," Peck declared, his bright, blue eyes popping over the rim of his glasses for the first time. "He's got metal studs in his head like a mohawk, and he likes to cut on people. He's a fan of razor blades."

Awww shit, I thought to myself. "And what are we gonna do?"

"We gotta be very careful with this one," Peck pooched out his lips and drew some coffee. He swallowed the hot fluid with a grimace. "This motherfucker has one basic way of enforcing things."

"Uh huh. And what's that?"

"He's simple," Peck said seriously. "He's old school. He just cuts your dick off."

I grimaced.

"You wouldn't believe how many dickless men are running around this island."

"Okay, I'm outta here," I stood up.

"Don't be a little bitch!" Peck screamed. Everyone looked. I sat back down.

"You're gonna be fine," he reassured me. "If anybody loses a dick, it'll be me. You're just there to back me up. I would never put you in the line of fire; you're not trained."

I sat back down. "This whole thing doesn't feel right," I shivered.

"Hey, hey. Look amigo," Peck now addressed me like a wise man. "You hit the lottery. You can get your life back on track now. Make a fucking decision man! RIGHT NOW! Are you with me or not? Okay? Just chill."

I kicked back and looked at the puffy white clouds slowing drifting across the bluest sky I had ever seen. For some reason I trusted this warped man. "Okay, so what's the plan then?"

Peck smiled. "Let's take the check, go somewhere else, and I'll tell you."

* * *

Peck took us outside El Morro, the island's dominant cliff fortress, to the sweeping, emerald-green, grassy field that overlooked a historic cemetery below. The graveyard was studded and riddled with gothic, chalky-white tombs rising up in a chaotic grid. In the distance, crystal-blue waves crashed on the rocks in a chaotic, frothy, unforgiving undulation; same as they'd done for eons. Each wave clashed like a cymbal, and the soothing, Caribbean wind whipped through my hair as fifty or more colorful kites flew and hovered in the heavens above, piloted by mesmerized children and their loving families. And in this peacefulness, here we were—two twisted birds plotting in the background, worried about our dicks.

"Here's the deal," Peck said, leaning back and absorbing the sun and wind like a lizard. "Things are not the way you think they are."

"I've already figured that part out," I said.

Peck laughed, and collapsed onto the grass, taking in the solar waves of energy. "Do you really believe in aliens?" he said, half-interested in my response.

I thought about his question for a moment. "Yes, yes I do. The universe is a big place. One time I read that there are more stars in the universe than there are grains of sand on all the beaches in the world."

This statement energized Peck and he bolted upright. "Yes! Yes amigo. That's the deal."

"So what do you know?" I asked sincerely.

"Well," Peck responded, lying back down, "Since 1947 the U.S. government has been working with the . . ." he hesitated "visitors . . . and they've been getting along rather well. A lot of that work has been done right here, in Puerto Rico, in the middle of the Bermuda Triangle, where time and space converge on a level that makes it easier for inter-stellar travel and communication to occur. And that is the crux of our problem." Oh great I thought; suddenly he's scientist now. "You keeping up with me?"

"Yeah," I said.

"The US government has bases all over Puerto Rico—the chosen destination for the ETs—the oldest land in the entire Caribbean, where the ETs had their first bases set up. All was good until two years ago. That's when the head drug dealer on the island kidnapped the ET ambassador, and then everything fucked up." He was silent for a while.

"So," I said, "a drug dealer kidnapped an alien?"

"Yes, amigo. They kidnapped this alien and are black-mailing the US government; using this little bastard to keep their drug trade flowing through Puerto Rico, to the states. Uncle Sam doesn't want it known, so as long as the scum-lords here on the island have the alien, the kingpins are free to peddle their wares."

I thought for a minute, closing my eyes in the hot sun. "Man, this sounds like a bunch of bullshit."

"And so, amigo," Peck continued, "I am here to take out the drug dealer infrastructure, man-by-man, until they release our little friend."

This all sounded to me exactly the way it probably sounds to you right now. "O . . .kay," I replied. "And why is this alien so important?"

With that, Peck raised up and grabbed my leg. It was a bit unnerving, since it was the first time he'd physically contacted me so directly. "What the fuck do you mean!" he exclaimed. "He's a goddamn alien! And not just any alien! Because amigo! This alien—the one that has been taken hostage—is the most intelligent being in the universe."

For a few moments, we just sat there and looked at each other. I spoke. "The drug dealers have kidnapped the most intelligent being in the universe, and you're . . ." I had to think about how to word this ". . . applying pressure to get him back?"

"Yeah amigo, yeah--exactly," Peck nodded, satisfied, then laid back down in the sun.

We just rested there quietly for a long time, and I thought about what was happening. My gut told me not to believe any of this. But, honestly, there was another part of me that wanted it to be true. Like everybody I know, I've been struggling and disappointed my whole life. I've seen the shows, read the books, looked at the crap on the internet, and hoped there really was something more going on. Maybe this was it. Maybe not. But before I met this weirdo, I had nothing planned, and that was stressful, too. Now, at least there was something, and maybe a chance to get things back on some kind of track in my life. I was getting too old to just keep lying and running. Sometimes I wanted to go back to Tennessee and find a hot girlfriend. Puerto Rican ladies weren't into me.

* * *

That night, the narrow lanes were filled with people, party lights flashing from the windows. Drunken Spanish chatter bounced off the old walls of San Sebastian Street. Men passed with waves of cologne and slick hair. Women in short skirts clicked by on high heels, ankles wobbling on the stone crevices. Peck and I stood before Oscuro, a happenin' cantina, young people spilling out the doors. The bar inside was backlit in dim blue, and liquor bottles lined the walls. Music blasted. It was hard to tell what kind of music played, since it morphed into the other beats of the nightlife.

"Are you ready?" Peck grinned.

"Yeah," I answered unenthusiastically.

The two of us wandered through the doorway, gringo snowmen in a shady cove of fresh, dancing Puerto Ricans. The bartender who spied us first was a big guy, late-20s, with tough skin, a mustache and goatee, and a black dew-rag tight around his head. The moment he laid eyes on us, he almost snickered. I could immediately tell this guy was an asshole. He was just waiting to see what awkward words would come from our mouths.

"Hola amigo," Peck said loudly, combatting the noise. The bartender just looked at him. "I would like a mojito please."

The bartender's snicker erupted into full condescension. "You want a what?"

"A mo-hi-to," Peck stressed the syllables.

The bartender chuckled and turned to another man

behind the bar, a smaller, monkeyish guy who was pulling some glasses from a cooler. "Hey," he called, "this guy wants a mojito!" They both shared a hearty laugh, then after glancing at me, he turned back to Peck.

"We don't have mojitos here amigo." His eyes were arrogant. "We just have hard liquor and good beer. This time of night, maybe go back to your cruise ship for one." The monkeyish guy laughed again and nodded his head.

"I'm confused, dude. What?" Peck replied. "What's happening here?" They continued to laugh at him dismissively.

Peck was quiet for a moment, then he walked to the side and around behind the bar. Just as the bartender's expression turned to surprise, Peck withdrew a shiny, 9mm pistol and pointed it at the bartender's head. Instantly, the bartender and his colleague lifted their hands and cowered back. The place was so noisy and active that no one else noticed what had happened.

"Oh, come on amigo!" Peck said. "I know you've got some mint and some rum and sugar and shit back there, so make me a mojito right now."

"Okay! Okay!" the bartender almost tripped backwards, scrambling for ingredients. The other man scurried away in fear. I stood in awe. I couldn't believe what I was seeing.

Cabinets were flying open, glasses were toppling over, and it looked like the bartender had eight arms. Peck kept his weapon trained on him. It was amazing to see how quickly a big dickhead transformed into a scared little man. The nearby customers were laughing their assess off, like this was obviously some kind of practical joke. Peck was totally at ease as mint was suddenly being squooshed and icy liquids were being combined.

"Muddle it! Muddle it right, motherfucker!" Peck commanded. In a minute or so, a beautiful mojito was on the bar; even the paper on the tip of the straw had a nice little twist.

Still brandishing his gun, Peck picked up the cold glass and took a long swig. The bartender almost held his breath.

"Yummm," Peck relished the taste. "Not bad amigo. Not bad," he said. He put the gun away, pulled a $20 bill from his pocket and put it on the counter. "You can keep the change amigo," he smiled. "That was definitely worth it." Peck slurped the rest down in a few seconds. "Muchas gracias," he called, as he motioned to me and we headed out the door.

As soon as we were on the street, we were walking away quickly.

"What was the point of that?" I asked.

"We have to fuck with 'em man," Peck replied.

I glanced back over my shoulder and upped my pace. "We're gonna get killed."

"No, we're fine," he said. "There are cops everywhere tonight. They're not gonna mess with us."

Five minutes later, we were a few streets down, near

the main square, Plaza De Armas. I was scanning the walkways around us constantly, expecting someone to come chasing us. It was a scary feeling. There were only people laughing, old bums lounging and vendors buzzing around in the romantic half-light, a fountain spilling in the middle.

"Okay," Peck said. "I'm pooped. Here." He handed me another $200. "Go get a good night's rest and meet me right here tomorrow, noon, for lunch. Sweet dreams amigo." Then he walked off.

The next afternoon we slipped into a dark corner of the Parrot Club, a nice lunch joint with an upscale Cuban atmosphere, right off Fortaleza Street. The waiter, prim in white apron, poured me a light, refreshing Medalla beer from the bottle. It usually came in a sweaty gold can, and was the local favorite. Before Peck, he placed the most glamorous, colorful, decorated margarita that a real man should never drink, but Peck was delighted as always. After placing our orders for a couple of Cuban sandwiches, I fiddled briefly with my cell phone, but I was eager to get down to business. Peck spoke first.

"So, Bill, what did you want to be when you grew up?" I was taken aback by the question.

"Well, actually, I kind of wanted to be a policeman."

"Oh, that's cool. What happened?"

"Oh, you know,"I stammered around some, "I needed money when I was a teenager. My mom and dad were always in and out of work, and we were poor. The guys I hung out with were roughnecks, so I started selling dope. And once that started, the cops sorta became my arch enemies."

"You ever sell anything other than weed?" Peck asked, thoroughly enjoying his flamboyant beverage.

"No, just bud. But since I've been here in Puerto Rico, I haven't been involved with any of that. I haven't even seen or heard about any drugs."

"Everybody on this island is doped up," Peck leaned in close.

"Well, I'm not," I stressed.

"Oh yes you are, dude," Peck assured me.

"What do you mean?"

Peck lifted his index finger into the air dramatically and slowly arched over, pointing down at my beer. "The Medalla," he whispered.

"Huh?"

"How long have you been here?" Peck asked.

"Uh, about a year and half I guess."

"And you've been all over the island?"

"Yes."

"And everywhere you go, everybody drinks Medalla, don't they?" he nodded knowingly.

"Well, yeah, pretty much," I said. "But it's hot and we're on an island, and people like to drink beer at the beach."

"But you see, Medalla is not just any beer," Peck

continued. "If you start asking around you'll find that everybody's drinking Medalla, but nobody knows anybody who works at the Medalla factory. Have you ever seen the Medalla factory?" He sounded almost like he was telling a ghost story now.

"No."

"The Medalla factory is in Mayaguez, on the other side of the island. It's big white towers of brew, surrounded by a fence and guards, and they don't let anybody in. It's like Willy Wonka's factory. Trucks go in and out under cover of night, and the drivers are men with no names. You know why?"

He definitely had my attention now. "Why?"

"Because Medalla is made by the government. And it's filled with chemicals to make the people here complacent. It blocks their perception of the UFO activity here. The people who don't drink the Medalla are dangerous. They can see things better. Some even hear voices. They are contacted by the aliens."

"And why are the aliens so into this place again?" I asked.

"It's the middle of the Bermuda Triangle, amigo. It's a portal, and they use it to fly back and forth between here and other dimensions. And the spiritual people here sense the visitors, and the visitors sense them, and the government just wants all the alien power, as usual."

"You've really got your conspiracies down pat, don't you?" I said, taking another swig of the Medalla.

He set back, satisfied with himself. "Conspiracies are real, amigo. Don't forget, the president had a blowjob conspiracy. Imagine what they do when it comes to important shit."

∗ ∗ ∗

That evening was like déjà vu. Once again, we were scoping out Oscuro. This time, the crowd was even bigger. We were much more hidden this time, observing from a point farther down the street.

"How is this gonna work," I asked impatiently.

"Well, you're gonna go in there and buy a mojito."

"And what are you gonna do?"

"I'm gonna stay right here and watch this," Peck said confidently.

"BULL SHIT," I replied. "What if they cut my dick off!"

"No, that wouldn't happen here," Peck reassured me. "They're on-guard tonight, just waiting for us to come back. And when you go in there, they'll kidnap you and take you to the Chupacabra's lair. And I'm gonna follow you, since I don't know where the fuck it is. And when we get there, I take care of business."

"This is ridiculous," I said. "What if you lose track of me and I'm on my own and they cut my fucking dick off?"

"I can't lose track of you amigo, remember? I've got a bug up your ass."

"Oh Jesus," my heart started pounding, and I rubbed

my sweaty brow. "Are you serious? You want me to go in there by myself and get kidnapped?"

"You'll be fine. They won't try to hurt you until you're at the lair. Just have another shot of rum and relax. You can do this. It's all good amigo, it's all good."

Ten minutes later, my liquid courage built, I wandered into the Oscuro feeling like a complete dipshit. The same brawny bartender was working, and he seemed slightly surprised to see me, yet not entirely.

"Where's your friend?" he asked.

"He's . . . not with me tonight," I said. "I just want a drink."

"Oh? And what is that?" He already knew the answer.

"I'd like a mojito please."

He stared at me for a moment with an odd look on his face. "You want a mojito?" he asked sincerely.

"Yes please," I replied sheepishly.

"No problem, amigo," he said. I could feel that he was continuing the previous night in his mind. He'd spent 24 hours re-living his embarrassment over and over again, re-imagining what he could and should have done to save face. And now was his chance to do it properly. I was SO FUCKED.

At that moment, an awful thought occurred to me. What if Peck had a heart attack and dropped dead? Or what if he got an urgent call to go off on a more important mission? Now I was beginning to see why he'd picked me for this dirty work. The dim blue light behind the bar began to swirl. I felt light-headed. I was SO FUCKED. They were going to cut my precious dick off.

I had zoned out. The next thing I knew, the mojito was on the counter in front of me. I felt sure it had been drugged. I glanced around for thugs. Nothing seemed out of place. The bartender looked at me and waited for me to sip. I felt telepathic. It was like the bartender was saying you can drink this, and we'll do this the easy way, or we can knock you in the head and drag you away. The choice is yours. Oh Jesus. Maybe it would just kill me, and end all of this. I've always had suicidal tendencies, but this was ridiculous. Oh Jesus. I sipped the fucking drink.

* * *

When I came to, I was in the trunk of a car. I have always been claustrophobic, so it was one of the worst experiences of my life. Dark. Hot. Cramped. My head banged up and down as the ground rumbled below. Thank Jesus I must have been knocked out for quite a while, 'cause it didn't take long for the car to stop and the trunk to open. My eyes were blinded by the flashlights. I was zip-tied, and strong men struggled to pull me out, slammed me around, and drag me over concrete steps. I was afraid they were gonna break a bone, and it hurt like hell. I could tell I was deep in the woods somewhere, a chorus of tiny coqui frogs chirped and whistled all around. I had never been so scared.

They dragged and threw me around mercilessly, like a heavy sack of potatoes, until I finally landed hard in a rickety wooden chair. I was in some kind of hut with old-fashioned industrial lamps hanging from the ceiling. It looked like the Vietnamese torture room from a Rambo movie. Three tall men moved objects around me to clear out space. My eyes focused on chains, knives, whips—the usual stuff—hanging from the walls. Additionally, freaky dolls and posters of demonic faces, tongues whipping out, set the décor. It was meant to freak me out, and it was working.

The men were silhouettes speaking to each other in Spanish. One leaned down to zip-tie me to the chair. His breath was hot and his beads of sweat dripped on my cheek. Once the tie was pulled tight, the men talked a little longer and then walked out the door, leaving me alone. I heard their vehicle start up, tires spin, and I saw their headlights wipe by as they turned around and drove off. Now it was eerily quiet; just me and the coquis. I thought I could also hear the faint rushing of water nearby.

I tried to stand up. That's when I realized the chair was bolted into the floor. It definitely seemed rickety, but rocking it around to break it apart was much harder than you'd think. With my hands and feet bound, and then secured to a bolted chair, I could never attain enough force and momentum to do much. I wobbled pitifully. You've seen this scene in movies a million times.

My claustrophobia was kicking in again, and I wanted

to get the FUCK outta there. I was moving and jiggling, grunting and groaning. Then, from outside a cracked window, I heard a familiar voice. "Calm down amigo, and just stay put." It was Peck.

"Oh, thank you Jesus," I exhaled.

"Don't try to escape," Peck's voice continued. "He'll be here in a minute. Shhhhhh . . ."

I cannot tell you how difficult it was to patiently wait for my torturer to arrive. I kept imagining all the horrible ways this whole thing could go wrong. I could hear a soft shower outside, a morning rain, as the twilight of daybreak barely lit the sky. Then I heard the dubstep music, a deep, distorted, electronic bass, rumbling the sides of the hut as it got closer. It made my stomach quiver, and I felt like I was gonna shit my pants as the vehicle pulled back up, blinding headlights shining in. The music shut off. I heard car doors open. Then the door to the hut opened, and there he was.

El Chupacabra was six feet tall, slim, white and shirtless. He wore black leather pants. There were tattoos all over him. His head was hairless, but sure enough, spikes, like a metal mohawk, ran down the center of his skull. His eyes were wild and bright green. There was something weird about his mouth, but I couldn't tell what it was at first. He just stood there looking at me. I shuddered. Mentally, I was screaming "PECK!!!"

The other three men entered, but they were like faceless grey figures compared to the striking image of the

Chupacabra. He walked up to me and leaned down. It took me a moment to realize what I was looking at. There were piercings all over him, but the strangest one was an open ring mounted just below his bottom lip. It held a round space open, like a window, so I could see some of his bottom teeth, even with his mouth fully closed. I had never seen that kind of body modification before.

His eyes were locked on mine. "What's your name?" he said. I smelled a strong stench of alcohol. His voice was kind of high-pitched with no accent. He was a gringo.

"Bill," I felt like a child.

"Bill what?"

"Smith," I lied.

The Chupacabra laughed, and the others chuckled along with him.

"Where is he?" the Chupacabra asked intently.

"I honestly don't know man. I swear to God," I replied.

"Do you know what happens if you don't tell me?"

I gulped. "No," barely escaped my lips.

He walked over to a black box on a nearby table, opened it, and took out a razor blade. "I'm going to remove your penis," he said calmly.

"PECK!!!!!!" I was screaming mentally.

"So tell me, where is he?"

"Please, please don't remove my penis," I begged. "He's probably nearby. He's probably gonna come looking for me, but not if you cut my dick off."

"Put him on the table," the Chupacabra demanded of

his men. Hairy arms were instantly upon me. In the mean-time, the Chupacabra had clicked on a stereo in the corner and doomy dubstep music blasted the tiny room. It was a nightmare.

They cut me free from the chair. Now only my hands and feet were still bound, and they hoisted me up on an old, heavy-duty wooden table. One of the men jerked my shorts down, and my penis pulled back like a turtle draw-ing into its shell. "PECK!!!!!!!!!!!!!!!!" my mind screamed.

The Chupacabra walked over and hovered for a sec-ond. "Hold him down," he said. I felt the cold blade of the razor on my beloved schlong.

"PECK!!!!!!!!!!!!!!" I screamed out loud this time, for real.

If one single millisecond more had passed, I would be a half-pound lighter right now. But, miraculously, that instant was when Peck burst in the door like a cowboy. With swift, beautiful timing, he fired four headshots. He hit each of the three thugs in the head, and each man's head became pink mist. But when his bullet hit the Chupaca-bra, a loud "ping!" whistled as it ricocheted off his metal mohawk. There was some blood, but a mere flesh wound. With lightning speed, the extremely fit Chupacabra had twisted the gun from Peck's hand and punched him back out the door. OH SHIT.

I heard Peck groan as punches landed. With hyster-ical carelessness, I jumped down from the table, my hands and feet still bound. I hopped to the door to see the Chupacabra on top of Peck, wailing away. Lying on his back, Peck, it seemed, was clearly overwhelmed, pulling his arms and legs into a ball, guarding his face. I realized they were at the top of a concrete staircase, leading down to a stream below. The steps were slick as rain continued drizzling.

Though I never cared for football, I hurled my confined body like a rocket, a tackler, and thrust all my weight into the Chupacabra. His body easily gave way, tumbling away down the wet, unforgiving steps. He screamed with each roll downward. My own face planted in the dirt, but I could see Peck quickly scramble to his feet. He grabbed me and pushed me upright, then raced down the steps.

From my new perspective, I could see the Chupacabra lying near the bottom of the steps, his face split on a concrete edge with black blood flowing out. He scampered to get up, half-conscious, hands slipping on the stones. In no time, Peck was upon him, shoving him further down to the rushing stream below. It was a beautiful waterway in the half-light, like a rainforest from an amusement park, with giant, glistening dark-green leaves leaning down and majestic rocks parting the swift, gray currents of a gulley.

Peck, hat ajar, kicked and shoved his disoriented enemy to the edge of the water, and leapt on him with the full force of his somewhat scrawny weight. Then suddenly, Peck's wiry frame looked extremely strong, his arms sinewy muscles of steel, shoving the Chupacabra's face into the water with all his might. His neck stretched, it looked like the drug dealer's head might pop off as he flailed and struggled uselessly under the determination of Peck's murderous power.

"Die! Die! Die!" Peck screamed, each time shoving his enemy's head deeper, further, and harder into the gushing stream. Muddy, I sat watching in sick amazement. Once the Chupacabra's body went limp, Peck was still not satisfied, pressing the face ever further into the water, killing the corpse ten times over. Eventually, when it was clear that no creature, however immortal, could still be alive, Peck finally flopped back, panting with exhaustion and relief. He looked up at me.

"Are you okay, amigo?"

"I think so."

Peck staggered up the steps, then suddenly turned, ran back down and kicked the shit of the Chupacabra's head. He then nonchalantly resumed his walk back up the steps toward me. Peck produced a pocket knife and cut the zip ties.

"Okay, we gotta get the fuck outta here fast," he said, pointing the way down a muddy trail that surely led to his car.

* * *

We drove for a long time in silence, heading west, on terrible, deserted back roads. There were some scratches and marks on both of us, but no serious injuries. All that had happened did not seem real.

"Good job back there, amigo," Peck said thoughtfully. "You saved me."

"Killing people doesn't bother you at all, does it?" I said flatly.

He didn't respond for a while, then he said, "You know what, amigo? One time, I saw the real chupacabra."

"Uh huh," I said. I was so exhausted.

"I was on a trail out in the woods near where we're gonna camp soon." His voice was slow. He was tired, too. "I came around a bend, and there he stood, four feet tall. Big, black eyes. Claws . . . And I remembered that one time I heard that if you see one, you should just freeze. And then you start to hum a nice soothing tune, like a little lullaby, and just back away. That's what I did. And suddenly there was this swirling burst of energy all around him, like the Tasmanian Devil, and then he just flew away, right straight up into the sky."

"We're gonna camp?" I asked.

"Yep, amigo. We're gonna get way back off the road and lie low for a while and sleep."

"I need to wash," I said. "There's blood on me from those guys you shot."

"There's a little bay we can wash in," he said.

Once we were far enough back into the woods, he

pulled over into some thick growth. The sun was shining nicely. Peck opened the trunk and removed a case. In a few moments, he had withdrawn what looked like a gigantic Frisbee. He tossed it on the ground and it instantly flopped around and sprung into a fully-formed 2-man tent.

"That was cool," I said.

"The water's over there," Peck pointed. "I have some candy bars and drinking water in the trunk. Let's get some rest. When we wake up I'll tell you about tomorrow."

"What's tomorrow?" I asked with dread.

"We're gonna try to kill The Pirate," he replied. "Good-night." Then he crawled right into the tent and collapsed.

3

The Pirate

When I woke up, it was dark and humid. Peck was snoring. I crawled out of the tent and breathed deeply of the night air. I had no idea what time it was. All my bearings on life were utterly gone. This was mosquito country, and I opened the trunk to dig around for some spray. We were heading toward a beach village called Boqueron. I used to party and drink there, and in the summer, we called bug spray the Boqueron cologne.

Peck crawled out of the tent, groggy. "Hey, give me some of that amigo," he said. His hat was off, and Peck scratched salt-and-pepper bushy hair bristling on his head. His stubble was the same color. "It's kind o' hot out here tonight," he said.

He saw the light of my cell phone illuminating my features. His right hand went up, partially shielding his eyes.

"Why are you always fucking around on your phone?" he asked, annoyed.

His question hit me the wrong way—almost pissed me off. Then quickly, I almost said simply, "I'm just looking at the news," but I knew that would sound too fake. I took a deep breath. "My mom is sick," I stated unemotionally. It made me feel sick to finally say it to someone.

Peck sat down and was quiet for a few moments. "What's wrong with her?" he squinted.

"She has cancer," I said. "And the only way I can see how she's doing is through this phone." I clicked off the screen and put it away.

In a little bit, my eyes adjusted to the blackness of night.

"It's dark as hell out here," I said.

Peck gazed up at the clear stars. "Aw man. There's no moon tonight." There was excitement in his voice.

"What does that mean?"

"This is Parguera. The water around here glows at night. Come here." Peck traipsed off through the weeds and I followed him into the darkness. When we reached the edge of the small bay beside us, it was still and shiny as a black mirror, a perfect reflection of the sprawling cosmos above. Peck ambled down into the water, and the instant his feet broke the surface, his lower legs were surrounded by electric neon-blue light. He reached down and scooped up a handful. It ran down his arms, twinkling all the way like little galaxies. He lifted another scoop and tossed it over the bay. It rained down and exploded into a thousand points of light as each droplet hit the surface. "That's what it looks like when it rains here."

I had heard of the bioluminescent bays of Puerto Rico, but never visited one. I was struck with a childlike sense of wonder and immediately waded into the dark water. An aura of light, like fluid from a blue glow stick, surrounded my entire body, and I couldn't help but smile ear to ear. I jumped and splashed around, bobbing up and down—a fireworks show all around me.

"Cool, huh, amigo?" Peck waded in deeper himself. "Some assholes say this part of the island doesn't glow much anymore. But you just have to hit when it's warm and dark, when the conditions are just right."

"What causes this?" I asked.

"Tiny little creatures," Peck held a handful right up to his eyes. "But the Spaniards thought it was the power of the devil. I think this is the real Fountain of Youth that Ponce De Leon was searching for."

The water was so warm and salty it felt like a big magical spa. I dove right in and swam out toward the middle. I felt free. I floated on my back for a while, staring up at the Milky Way, letting the therapeutic water swish in and out of my ears, taking me away from my troubled senses. The nightmare had become a surreal dream, and for a moment, I felt perfect. I would have laid there on my back the rest of the night, but as my head dunked out of the water here and there, I thought I heard a sound like shouting. I lifted upright, easily floating in a seated position, and I could hear clearly now. Peck was screaming at the shore.

"Oh shit! OH SHIT! Get out! Get the fuck out!!!"

I sighed. Never a moment's peace. What was it now? I twisted my body around in one smooth motion. What

I saw makes the hair stand up on my arms even as I write this now.

In the silent, coal-black water, just below the surface, a huge glowing, blue form glided around me. It was easily the size of a van, and streamlined in shape. Instant panic. I felt a jolt in my heart. Maniacally I beat the waves in some attempt at swimming. "Get the fuck out!" Peck kept screaming.

This was almost worse than a scene in JAWS. The whole situation was so foreign to usual human experience. This horror surely plucked the vulnerable strings of my ancient, primitive DNA—I felt like a tiny cuddly creature about to be swallowed by a behemoth hungry mouth. With adrenaline-powered fury, I somehow crossed an amazing distance of water in what seemed a few seconds. And when I hit the shore, I didn't stop. I just kept running till I slammed right into a tree, stubbed my toe, and nearly knocked myself out.

Peck was laughing like a madman. "What the fuck!" he kept looking out at the water. "That was AMAZING amigo!"

I groaned and pulled myself up from the soil.

"Are you okay, amigo?"

"Yeah," I held my head. "I just ran into a tree."

"That was wild, huh?" Peck continued to marvel, staring across the bay.

"What the hell was it?" I was desperate for insight.

"I don't know man," Peck said, bewildered. "It could

have been one helluva giant fish. Or it could be one of the USOs."

"What's a USO?"

"That's an Unidentified Submerged Object," he plopped down next to me. "It's like a UFO, but under the water. And sometimes they shoot right outta the water and fly away."

"Are they aliens, too?" I asked, SO relieved my heart was now beginning to calm.

"It depends," Peck replied. "I mean, this is Pargeura. This is the place where the government did a bunch of their wild experiments. This is where they brought the monkeys."

"The monkeys?"

"Absolutely amigo. In the late 1930s, just before WW2, the U.S. government built a little laboratory on a tiny island off the coast of Parguera. They brought monkeys over from India and did experiments on them that are still classified to this day. In the 1950s, just like a scene from a bad sci-fi movie, some of the monkeys escaped. And so now there are packs of giant, mutated monkeys that roam this part of the island. They're five fucking feet tall."

"No way!" I resisted. "I've never seen a monkey here before."

"I shit you NOT amigo," Peck stressed. "They're real smart, but they carry diseases. And one time they hired a sniper to come in here and shoot as many as he could every day. He got a lot of 'em, but there are still plenty around. But you know what I think amigo?"

"What's that?"

"I think the government took some monkeys, and some iguanas and some alien DNA, and played around and made chupacabras. Think about it. They're 4 feet tall and hunched like a monkey, they have claws and spines like an iguana, but they manipulate time and space like an alien. It all makes sense."

"So there are monkeys out here tonight?"

"Yeah. And a shitload of iguanas, too."

"Where are the iguanas?"

"They're in the treetops all above us."

I shuddered and looked up. "Seriously?"

"Yeah, amigo."

"Can they fall on us?"

"Sure, it's possible."

"I'm goin back into the tent," I said.

* * *

The next morning I smelled coffee. I opened the tent to see Peck, sitting on a log, preparing a pot of fine Café Rico brew over a small fire. It smelled great, so I slowly emerged, took a leak, then sat down on another log he'd dragged out to join him for a cup.

"Numbers is very happy that Chupacabra is dead," Peck handed me a hot mug.

"Really?" I said.

"Yes sir. They're gonna be really happy with you."

"Good," I said, barely sipping the steamy liquid. The morning was serene, soft light outlining each tree.

"And today," he gazed up triumphantly, "we will find El Pirata—the Pirate."

The thought of engaging another villain filled me with dread. "What is he like?"

"Talk about a real piece of shit," Peck shook his head. "The kind of scum a woman doesn't want to meet at night in a dark alley. He's a dirty, unkempt creep who likes to sell poison to school kids. One hundred hidden hands will try to stab us in the back the moment we enter his beach."

"Wonderful," I said, almost detached from the meaning of his words.

"Yeah, he thinks he's Cofresi. You know Cofresi?"

"Nope."

"Aw, dude, Cofresi was the big pirate around here back in the 1800s." I sensed storyteller mode coming on again. "He sold his soul to the devil so that men would fear him and women would love him. He used to take guys and nail 'em down on the deck of his ship to let 'em die of exposure. When he was finally captured by an American military ship, they took him to El Morro in San Juan and shot him. But right before he died, he uttered a curse on the ship that had taken him. Years later it sank, and everyone on-board died. Some locals think he's a Robin Hood-type hero, but our boy—the drug dealer—is all about the evil side. We gotta be careful with him since he has a lot of friends looking out for him."

"And what's the brilliant strategy to find him?"

"I'm not exactly sure yet. I think we'll just wander into Boqueron and start asking around."

Shit.

* * *

Boqueron was the same as always. It's a little fishing and beach village, full of charm and relaxation. Our convertible rolled through the streets in the afternoon, the sun glinting off the calm, picturesque bay, filled with small sailboats and yachts, as street vendors set up to sell their wares and foods. It reminded me of a little "Popeye" town more than any place I've ever been. Almost like a movie set, somewhat rickety and wooden, the air salty, twenty or so bars and restaurants lined the small area known as the poblado. Locals milled around, but at night, I knew the streets would be blockaded against cars, and the lanes would fill with hundreds of joyous people, drinking their stress away, eating, smiling and singing Karaoke. The balconies above would hold giddy, harmless drunks enjoying the show below. This was where Puerto Ricans came to enjoy themselves, especially on the weekends.

We parked in the shade of a wide alley, and hopped out into the warm breeze. It was a perfect day. The old street, made of criss-crossed bricks, gave an almost colonial air to the tiny town. I almost fell back in time, losing myself in fond memories there. Then I remembered why we'd come.

"How, how are we gonna find him?" I whispered to Peck. He stopped walking. "You said he has friends around every corner."

"Yes," Peck replied somberly. "That's right amigo. But we're just gonna have to be bold here. I mean, I'm not a fuckin' ninja and neither are you. So we just have to take the opposite approach. But if I ever say the word 'wee-wee' to you, I want you to instantly, without hesitation, start beating the shit out of whoever we're talking to. Okay?"

"Wee-wee?"

"Yes. That's the code word here, amigo. 'Wee-wee.' Okay?"

"All right," I said. By now I'd learned asking too many questions was a waste.

We passed a mangy pitiful mutt and strolled over to a quaint, inviting little bar, right by the water. You could tell it was a favorite hangout for the locals. Though it was still early, most were already laughing and staggering around. Each experienced drinker held a foam coozie, nursing a cold Medalla. They looked at us with curiosity, but no alarm, as we entered smiling dumbly and sat at the far end of the bar on broken down stools.

We'd walked right into the middle of an alcoholic debate, and one short, older, glassy-eyed man, scruffy with a cigarette-wrecked voice, immediately tried to draw us in. "Let's ask these guys," he slurred, stumbling closer. "How does a blind man know when to stop wiping his ass?"

Everyone chuckled and looked at us. I looked at Peck. He flashed his usual winning grin. "That is a damn good question amigo," he said. "I donno. Maybe when his seeing eye dog stops licking?"

The whole bar howled with laughter, and it seemed like we had, sure enough, broken the ice.

"Where are you from?" the drunk asked.

"North Carolina," Peck said innocently.

"Are you on vacation?"

"Yeah, we are."

The bartender, a wise weathered lady, with short white hair and twinkling eyes asked "What can I get you to drink?"

"I'd like a mojito," Peck said.

"We don't make mojitos," she replied.

Oh fuck. Here we go again. But no . . .

"That's okay," Peck smiled. "How about a rum punch then?"

"Rum punch," she said. "Okay. And you?" she looked at me.

"Uh . . . I'll just have a Medalla," I said.

"Oh, and I'll have a chichaito shot, too," Peck added.

"What flavor?" she asked.

"How about nutella?" Peck's face lit up.

The drunk stumbled closer. He looked back and forth between my beer and me.

"So you like to meditate?" he asked.

"I'm sorry?" I responded.

"Meditate," he stressed. "You like to meditate?"

"Uh, not really," I said, a bit confused.

"Cause you know how we meditate here?"

I didn't know where this was going. "How?"

"Like this," he put his hands together and closed his eyes in a solem pose. "Ummmmmm . . ." he hummed like a monk. I noticed the others around him start to chuckle and roll their eyes like they'd seen this routine before. His voice went up in volume. "Uuuummmmmmm . . ." The snickers around the bar continued. Then his mantra shifted to "UmmmmmmmmmmmmMeedalla." Everyone laughed including me and Peck.

He sniggered, proud of himself, then asked earnestly, "So where ya been?"

"Oh, well we were at the bio bay."

The drunk's eyes lit up. "Oh man, that bio bay is amazing. Ya know, if you go out there late at night you can see glowing fucking dolphins leaping through the air. It's fucking beautiful."

"No shit!" Peck slapped the bar. "Glowing dolphins? You gotta be kidding me amigo!"

"Yeah, seriously," the drunk fished a smoke from his pocket. "But you gotta be careful if you get in the water 'cause they'll rape you."

"Bullshit!" the bartending lady exclaimed.

"No! Seriously. They will! I know two guys who have been raped by those fucking things. Bert and Ken."

"Well I've never heard that before," the bartender said.

At that point, a strange figure entered the shabby room. It was a young man, perhaps in his 20s, with dark hair and a faint mustache. He moved in awkward, jagged spurts, obviously disabled. His eyes were out of whack, and he passed us then struggled to find a seat at the opposite end of the bar. The room quietened down a bit. The drunk glanced at us, then leaned closer.

"That's Roberto. That boy was hit in the head by a coconut."

"Oh my God," Peck said, feigning concern.

"Yeah, his dad used to be a tree trimmer. And when you get hit in the head with a coconut it's like a fucking bowling ball falls on you. He's been hit three fucking times. I won't stand near him."

"Three times!" Peck could barely conceal his surprise.

"Yeah, seriously," said the drunk. "The first time it almost killed him. The second time, he kind o' straightened up for a while. But then the third time he was fucked up again. He's a good boy, but just unlucky as hell."

The bartender brought our drinks.

"Oh lovely. Thank you," said Peck, admiring his new pink concoction. I cracked open the beer.

"Well guys, I gotta go," the drunk said. "Nice meetin' ya." He shook our hands and shuffled away. Most of the men in the bar followed him.

"So," Peck said to the bartender, "what's your name?"

"Aja," she said.

"I'm Dick," he extended his hand. They shook.

"So Aja," he said, "I'm supposed to meet El Pirata. Where is he at?"

Aja instantly stiffened. "Who are you again?" she asked suspiciously.

"Oh," Peck perked up. "I'm a friend of Margarita."

She looked at him for a moment, doubt on her face, then said "I'll be right back." She stepped into a back room.

"Who's Margarita?" I whispered to Peck.

"I donno," he said. "On this island, nine times outta ten, if you say you know Juan or Margarita, it'll work out." I closed my eyes and shook my head.

A few minutes later, Aja came back. "I'm sorry," she said resolutely. "I don't know."

"You don't know where he is?" Peck pressed.

"I'm sorry," she said. "I can't help you." Then she turned and walked into the back once again.

The two of us sat there in silence for a while. The only other person at the bar was the coconut boy, and Peck turned his attention to him. With great ease, Peck stood and walked over, then sat down beside him. I stayed put, but could hear what he said next.

"Hola amigo," Peck extended a hand. The coconut boy flashed a crooked grin and shook. "Your name is Roberto?"

"Yep," his voice sounded weird.

"Well my name is Dick."

"Okay."

"Yeah," Peck sipped his drink, "I'm a friend of the Pirate."

"Oh, I like pirates," Roberto said.

Peck smiled and nodded. "Yeah, where is he?"

"I like pirates," Roberto repeated.

"Do you now?"

"Yeah, I like pirates."

"Okay," Peck got up and moved back onto the stool next to me. "We just gotta feel this one out," Peck said to me.

"Pirates!" Roberto exclaimed with a goofy laugh.

"Well Bill," Peck said, sounding somewhat defeated, "we're in for a long day. I can tell."

"Pirates! Pirates!" Roberto shouted at the end of the bar.

"Yes," Peck humored him with a smile. "Pirates!"

"It's probably gonna be hard to find this motherfucker," Peck turned his attention back to me. "He avoids public exposure."

"Pirates!" Roberto shouted again, this time pointing across the street.

"Yeah, pirates are cool," Peck called down the bar.

"Pirates!" Roberto stood up, enthusiastically pointing across the street.

We looked out the entrance at another small bar on the other side of the lane, and I saw the back of a tall, slim man with long, black hair walk inside. He had a few guys with him.

"Pirates!" Roberto jumped up and down.

"Holy shit; that's him," Peck said, losing all interest in his rum punch.

"What? Are you sure?" I said.

"Holy donkey dicks," Peck replied, mesmerized. "Yep. That's our man. That's our fucking man."

I stood up.

"No, just stay calm," Peck said. "We'll settle our tab then go over there. Just be cool and finish your drink."

I had the jitters in my stomach, but I suppressed them and acted natural. My beer was gone in two seconds though. Aja reappeared.

"How much do we owe you?" Peck asked.

She looked at our drinks. "Four dollars." Peck laid down a five.

"Keep the change, senora."

Aja noticed that we had seen the man across the street. "Gracia," she said, and with a disapproving look she swiped up the bill and vanished quickly.

Peck sucked down his drink.

"Pirates! Pirates!" Roberto was excited.

"Yeah, yeah—thanks again amigo," Peck said, his focus now trained elsewhere. He looked at me. "Let's go."

We slowly walked out of the bar, heading over to the other side. Man, could it really be this easy? What in the hell was Peck gonna do? And then, BOOM, two young, big, Puerto Rican guys, wearing t-shirts and jeans came out of nowhere.

"Can I help you?" one said aggressively. They stormed toward us, hands already balled into fists. My stomach sank.

"Yeah," Peck said. These men looked angry and intense,

and they were focused on Peck. "I need some help with this." In a flash, Peck, this crazy bastard, had unzipped his pants and pulled his floppy white dick out.

"Eeew," the thugs cringed, drawing back, focus destroyed.

"Wee-wee," Peck said calmly. "Wee-wee."

This was clearly my window. Fighting instinct overwhelmed me. I kicked one guy's right knee out and he screamed. I dove and punched the other one in the throat. They both went down hard, and the entire village knew what was happening. I looked up and saw the Pirate for the first time. He dashed from the bar frantically. He was dressed in a white shirt with black jeans and leather boots. His eyes, eyebrows, mustache and goatee were black, as was that long hair. This guy did look like a pirate. And he brandished a pistol in his hand. Spanish words exploded in the background behind him, and people were dodging away and hitting the ground. He hesitated for a split-second, and I could tell he was thinking of shooting us. But Peck withdrew his pistol, and the Pirate ran like hell. For whatever reason, Peck chose not to chase him.

Peck jumped down on top of the guy I'd kicked in the leg. He jammed his shiny 9mm in the man's mouth. I could hear a tooth chip.

"I'm gonna kill you motherfucker," Peck looked him in the eye. "I'm gonna blow your fucking head right off if you don't tell me where he's going." I actually thought the man on the ground was gonna cry.

"Prrrto RRRll!" he said, the barrel distorting his words.

"What!" Peck spat in his face. "What!" he removed the barrel.

"Puerto Real! Puerto Real!" the man gasped.

Peck slammed the man's head down on the hard bricks, cracking his skull. "Let's go!" he said to me. We ran amidst a small crowd of shocked and terrified people, jumped into the convertible and hauled ass.

"Where are we going?" I asked.

"Not far. Puerto Real," Peck replied as we peeled out. We were zipping around curves and weaving in and out of traffic, blasting out of Boqueron. Puerto Ricans are loco drivers, so this was a little payback.

"Are we gonna catch him?" I shouted over the wind.

"No way," Peck shook his head. "He's probably on a motorcycle. But I'm not trying to catch him right now, just see where he's going." My heart leapt from my chest as Peck slammed on the brakes. We almost screeched into a horse trotting down the road. There was no rider and no explanation, but it was typical for this part of the island. Peck gunned it again.

Within a few minutes, Peck had turned up a hill, then rumbled across the deep ruts of an uneven dirt road. It sounded like it might tear the bottom of his car apart. We bounced up and down, ripping through leaves and branches. Then, a chorus of angels sang as we topped the mound, and a scenic vista of beautiful, blue coastline extended before us down below.

Peck jumped out, opened the trunk and pulled out a pair of giant binoculars. He pointed down below. I could see a clutter of little boats lining the shore. Behind them a dingy wooden town, weather-beaten boards, rustic and washed out in color.

"Down there is where he'll be docked somewhere," Peck said.

"Are you gonna shoot him from here?" I asked.

"No. Way too far for that. I'd probably miss. I'm just gonna see where he's going."

We waited for five or so minutes, and then I heard Peck go, "Oooh, oooh! There you are motherfucker!"

Even without the binoculars, I could see the Pirate's scraggly figure quickly run out to a boat, undock it, flip some switches and pull away.

"Ha, ha, ha! Of course! Look!" Peck thrust the binoculars into my hands.

I could see the little white yacht more clearly now as the Pirate churned out farther into the water.

"Yep," I said.

"Do you see what it says on the side?"

"Mmmm . . . No I can't really make it out."

"El Mosquito!" Peck exclaimed with delight, as he pulled the binocs away from me.

"So what?"

"That was the name of Cofresi's boat. I told you this guy believes he's the reincarnation."

"And you're just gonna watch him sail away?"

"That's all I need to see," Peck said. "His drug lab won't be further than 3 miles from Puerto Real. Any beyond that, and the corrupt local lawmen couldn't protect him. He's heading northwest. There are only a few islands out there that could support his little factory." Peck continued watching until the Pirate was no more than a tiny dot on the sunlit horizon.

He put the lenses away and pulled out a detailed map, unfolding it on the trunk, sprawling in all directions.

"Ahhh," Peck said. "I bet it's this little fucker," he pointed at a small blob off the coast. "I think it's called Lizard Island." He stood there contemplating for a bit.

"So we're gonna go there? To his island?" I asked with concern.

"Yeah, but quietly. We'll get close by and hide out. Then we'll wait for sundown, and we'll be able to see his lights. You're a good swimmer man, don't worry."

"Swimmer!" I was unnerved. "What does swimming have to do with this?"

"We can't take a boat over there, amigo. We've got to creep in like James Bond. I've got some snorkels."

"Aww, man, this is bullshit," I said. "How are we gonna get off the island?"

"We'll just take one of his boats. Don't sweat it amigo. It'll all work out. I have a friend here who can help us. Let's go."

＊　＊　＊

Thirty minutes later, we were outside a broken-down house with dogs barking and roosters crowing. A tanned Puerto Rican walked out with a big smile. He was in his late 40s, fit, with a little mustache. He wore a black, silly-looking visor hat with fake, gray hair sprouting wildly from the top.

"Amigo!" he screamed with robust joy, embracing Peck. "Amigo!"

Peck screamed back, hugging him tightly. There was a chorus of "Amigo!" that went on for a minute or more.

"This is my friend Bill," Peck finally introduced me. We shook, and the man shined his kind eyes at me. "Bill this is Eduardo, my fishing buddy."

"Good to meet you," Eduardo smiled with broken English.

"He's a fisherman around these parts," Peck explained. "And," he looked at Eduardo, "I need your help amigo."

"Okay," he said. "No problem. Come have a beer."

We lounged in his backyard, cluttered with boat parts. Eduardo and I and sipped cold Medallas, but Peck chose a Coors Light.

"We need you to drop us off close to Lizard Island," Peck said.

"Okay," Eduardo seemed agreeable. "And why is that?"

"I have some spying to do."

"Oh," Eduardo replied. "I see. I try to stay away from that area. But you must be looking for El Pirata?"

"That's right amigo. I'll pay you for the trip."

"Okay," Eduardo nodded. "There are lots of little islands out that way, so I'll drop you off somewhere. And when do you want me to pick you up?"

"That won't be necessary amigo. We'll catch a ride back. Just let me leave my car at your place."

"Are you sure about that Peck?" I interjected.

"Yeah, we'll be fine amigo. This'll all work out just fine."

*   *   *

The balmy wind felt great as we bounced across the sea on Eduardo's little fishing boat. By now, the sun was starting to wane a bit. I felt like I was being rocked to sleep, reminded of how little good rest I'd gotten the night before.

"There is a whole little chain of islands out here near Lizard Island," Eduardo called. "How close do you wanna be?"

"Not too close. Slow down," Peck instructed. Eduardo eased off the throttle and the engine quietened.

"We're sneaking over there by snorkeling," Peck clarified.

"Oh really?" It seemed the insanity of this idea hit Eduardo.

"Yeah, we'll be fine."

"So how close? That's Lizard Island there," Eduardo pointed. We could barely see a dark spot in the distance. A chain of cays dotted the water between us and the island.

"Just pull over right up here," Peck directed.

I jumped into the warm, aquamarine crystal-clear water and helped Eduardo anchor down the boat in the underwater sand. Once we were set up, Eduardo took off his shirt, revealing a hairy, grey chest, climbed down into the sea, and swam around like a fish.

"Ohh, is nice!" he grinned. "Is like a big swimming pool!"

All three of us took a moment to swim and play around. It felt incredible. Even swimming for fun, Peck still wore his sunglasses and hat. He looked like a dork.

"So you sure about this?" Eduardo asked, genuine concern in his voice.

"Oh yeah, amigo, we're all good," Peck reassured him.

Eduardo handed down Peck's waterproof pack. "And you have you sandwiches and sunblock and bug spray, and you gun?"

"Yeah, yeah, yeah," Peck dismissed the concern. "We're set, man. This is gonna be easy peezy Japaneezy."

"All right," Eduardo said climbing back onto the boat. "If you going to snorkel over there, you better get started before it's dark. You got my cell number so call if you have trouble."

"Ok amigo, I will."

"Nice to meet you," Eduardo called down to me.

"You, too. Thanks!" I said.

And with that, Eduardo, our only real friend out there, our only real hope, was puttering away in the distance, waving back at us, a pure white trail of bubbles behind him. It crossed my mind that this may be the last friendly thing I would ever see.

"Let's wade up to the shore," Peck said. A couple minutes later, we were sitting on the tiny beach. Peck reached into his gear pack and pulled out two sets of mask, fins and snorkel. "We're just gonna quietly make our way over there," he said. "But we won't go on shore until after dark. Then we'll snoop around and figure out where they are."

"All right."

"But be real careful when you're snorkeling," he said.

"Don't worry. I've snorkeled before."

"Yeah, but there's fire coral all around here." He stuffed his hat and glasses in his pack.

I furrowed my brow. "What is that?"

"Aw man," Peck said. "It's a coral that glows bright red like hell itself. And if you touch it, it'll blister you. You don't wanna know what it's like to touch fire coral."

There it was, another lump of fear in my throat.

"Let's go," Peck said.

"Wait a minute!" I called. "So this fire coral is just red and you don't touch it and that's all?"

"Right."

"Is there anything else I need to know?"

"No amigo. Just the usual crap. Don't touch the giant jellyfish and shit. I mean, basically, don't touch anything."

"Are there . . . a lot of sharks around here?" he could hear the note of concern in my voice.

"You know something, amigo," he paused. "That brings

up a very interesting factoid. Did you know that never, in recorded history, has there ever been one single shark bite on the western side of the island? Not once. In fact, only two people have ever been killed by sharks in Puerto Rico, and those both happened around San Juan in the 1920s. But here, on this side of the island, we are absolutely safe. Nobody seems to know why exactly. It probably has to do with the food chain or something. They probably don't have the kind of stuff sharks like out this way. But you can literally chum the water at night with a bucket of blood, and lay out there, floating around in it hanging your juicy ass down, and you'll still be fine. Now let's go." With that, he shoved off. I fumbled to strap on my gear, then shove off into the gorgeous water. Now it felt like a beautiful siren, calling me down to my doom.

The craggy reefs below were breathtaking. They teemed with colorful schools of fish, darting left and right as we foreign spacemen glided through. Once in a while, I hovered over a plump giant starfish, orange and planted firmly in the thick sand. Another time, a purplish octopus rolled his arms and scampered away. This was a world of wonder, and yet, once in a while, we raised our heads to take our bearings, and I was reminded of the death that loomed on the small isle ahead.

Occasionally, we drifted to a spot of land to rest, and then slipped back into the sea. On several occasions I spotted the bright-red coral, and frantically flailed as far as I could around it. But as the sun went down, the sights below us became more and more murky and spooky. As the final rays of light angled and beamed down through the sea, my eyes shot to the left and my heart raced. A six-foot long, pike-shaped fish, with the underbite of a piranha, quietly streamed through the water next to me. I froze, and it simply carried on, slipping ahead and away. Finally, we stopped on a cay so close to Lizard Island that I felt I could throw a baseball and hit our target.

"We'll rest here and watch the sunset," Peck said.

"I'll tell you one thing," I wiped the saltwater from my eyes. "There may not be sharks around here, but I saw a big-ass barracuda."

"Yeah," Peck smiled. "They're cool though. They're very friendly."

I stared over at Lizard Island, but saw no sign of man. "Are you sure this is the right place?" I asked.

"No," Peck panted, streams of saltwater dripping from his hair. "I'm not sure yet. But we'll know after the sun goes down."

An hour later, we were dry. The sun had died and Peck pulled a couple granola bars from his pack. "Here's dinner, amigo."

I eagerly tore open the packaging and scarfed down the meager food. He produced a bottle of water and I sucked the whole thing down in damn near one gulp.

"Look," Peck pointed. "Do you see it?"

I strained my eyes. Sure enough, I saw a golden light glint between the trees of Lizard Island.

"They're over there on the other side," Peck sounded confident. "They're cooking up meth and God knows what."

"How are we gonna handle this?" I asked.

"We'll go over and quietly scope things out. Then, when they go to sleep, I'll shoot them all."

"All right," I said. "So why am I here."

Peck rolled his eyes. "To keep me company."

Great.

＊ ＊ ＊

It was slow going, softly snorkeling over toward Lizard Island. We didn't want to splash too much. The current was getting a bit stronger though, and it was a little scary at times, feeling I was making no progress as I swam, gradually being pulled away in the infinite blackness. But little by little, we progressed. And eventually, exhausted, we carefully dragged ourselves onto the sharp gravel that rung the hard beach of Lizard Island. We both laid for a good ten minutes, the small tide softly whishing in and out around our bodies.

"Okay," Peck sat up. "Take off all your shit and let's get it back in the pack."

We spent a few minutes re-organizing. By the time we'd finished, I noticed just how good and dark it was. The stars were showing nicely above.

"There's a lotta shit to trip on in the dark, so we just gotta take our time and slowly make our way toward the light," Peck told me. "We're better off to stay near the shore. There's less growth and it's a little more noisy."

I nodded affirmatively.

This phase of our plan was especially long and laborious. But as we felt our away around rocks, logs and debris, more of the lights revealed themselves, and sure enough, I could hear Spanish words through the trees. There was an encampment there. I kept thinking we should stop, but Peck continued motioning us forward. We were finally so close that I could see a dozen silhouettes moving around a fire and numerous tents. Most of the men had long hair. I found it impossible to tell which one was the Pirate.

We laid on the ground and Peck put his lips right up to my ear. "Okay amigo," he barely spoke. "We just chill out here till they sleep, then we'll go over there and start killing these fucks."

"Okay," I whispered back.

The hours that followed were some of the longest of my life. And yet, it didn't really bother me. The sky was so clear, the moon so dark, that the stars twinkled mystically. I'd never been forced to lie on my back and stare up for so long. It was like a meditation, some kind of communion, that brought infinite ease and calm into me. In the background, I eventually heard things wind down. Twelve voices turned to six. Six to three. Three to two. Then there was one fellow moving things around. Once in a while, I could see the glow on his face as he checked a cell phone. Then finally, he went to bed.

I whispered to Peck, "If you start shooting into the tents, they might kill you."

"Don't worry amigo," he replied. "They're drunk. It won't take me but a minute to shoot every goddamn one of them."

An hour later, Peck whispered, "Let's go."

Very slowly and meticulously, we began moving across the uncooperative landscape. Every footfall was terrifying loud, and each time a twig broke, my heart skipped a beat. We got amazingly close to their camp, then a surprise: a dog started barking like hell. I jumped outta my skin and froze. Peck froze, too. It must have been fifteen minutes before that dog shut the fuck up, but it seemed like forever. When it finally did, we laid there another fifteen before Peck motioned for us to retreat. Just as slowly and pain-fully as we had approached, we took over an hour to make our way back to the island shoreline.

"Well, son-of-a-bitch," Peck spat in frustration. "I guess we have to do this differently. If that dog wakes them up, then we're pushing our luck a little too far."

"Think we should wait till morning?" I asked.

"Yeah," Peck resigned himself to the situation. "We'll wait for another opportunity to ambush them when I can see them but they can't see me."

"So I guess we're sleeping right here tonight?"

"That's right amigo, if you can sleep."

* * *

I don't know if you could really call it sleep, but something took me away, and when my eyes opened, the sun was up, and Peck was leaned against me snoring, his 9mm in hand.

"Peck," I nudged him.

"Huh?" he woke up. He was startled for a wild-eyed moment, but then immediately back in the situation.

"Yeah amigo," his breath was bad. "You okay?"

"Yeah, I'm fine. What are we gonna do?"

Peck cleared his throat and looked back over toward the camp. "We're just gonna hang out here till they get up."

"Well hopefully that's soon, huh?"

"Right, yeah," he closed his eyes, rolled over, and went back to sleep in the sand.

* * *

"Ahhh!" I was slapping everywhere. Something had crawled on me. It was hot as fuck, and when I opened my eyes, a tiny, brown little lizard raced away. He paused after a few moments, stone still at first, then began waving his tail around like a fine whip. The sun was directly overhead. I heard Peck snoring.

"Peck!" I shook him awake.

"Yeah, yeah, amigo," he shot up.

"Wake up. It's noon."

He sat up and gathered himself. Thank goodness we had mainly been in the shade.

"Yeah," he said. "They're still asleep over there," he craned his neck around toward the camp. "I've been up every half hour, and they're still sleeping."

"My back hurts," I said. It felt like the vertebrae between my shoulder blades had been crushed into a ball. "What's the plan. This sucks."

"Yep," Peck stretched. "Let me take a piss, then we'll slip around the shore and see where their boats are."

We both took a leak, then slowly made our way around the island. The sun was so bright the blue water was blinding. Once we passed a little point, we could see three boats docked. Two of them were small and one was a bit larger. The big one had twin engines on the back.

"That's probably where they're hiding the drug cargo," Peck said. He unzipped his pack, and put his familiar hat and sunglasses back on. "These lazy assholes might sleep till 3pm. Let's go over and see what their cargo is."

"You wanna get on their boat?" It seemed like a crazy idea to me.

"Yeah," Peck replied. "I wanna see what they've got."

We shoved through the bright, waist-deep water till we were right next to the three boats bobbing up and down in the water. El Mosquito was a small one. The largest one was called Santa Cofresi. We pulled our wet asses up the ladder of the Santa Cofresi, and were shortly on board. The white deck was hot. A compartment was open to a dark area below. Peck pointed to the opening downward. He walked down first. I followed into the blackness, watching my movement on the narrow steps.

It was unimaginably dark, hot and stuffy. When my eyes adjusted, I could see large bundles of plastic wrapped with cords.

"This is it," Peck mumbled. "There's a shitload here."

Just then, we heard a voice above speaking Spanish. I looked at Peck. He pulled out his gun, and we just stared at each other a moment. Then we could feel someone step on-board. Peck frantically pointed to an area at the back of the cargo hold. We both crept into the dark space, squeezing between the bails of drugs, hiding like frightened animals.

Soon the voices above were joined by other voices. It was clear that they were boarding the boat. At any moment, someone could enter the cargo hold and see us. Then we heard a struggle of some kind. A shadow fell over the steps leading down toward us. We cringed as we watched two men pull another heavy load down the narrow steps, entering our space. I looked at Peck. He looked at me. It was obvious that this could be the end. We watched a man's hunched form, entering the cargo hold and straining to drag a large bundle down with him. Someone was obviously pushing on the other end. I held my breath.

"Mios Dios!" the man panted. He shoved the load back in our direction, pushing it with his foot. Then he wiped his brow and walked back up the steps. At that point, we heard and felt the footsteps of more men boarding above us. Peck looked at me with a profound seriousness. I realized we were now along for the ride.

I lost track of time, but in retrospect, I'd say we were down there a good hour before the engines cranked up and the whole boat began to vibrate. Then it was another fifteen minutes or so until I sensed the motion of the boat backing out. The feet on the deck above us kept walking back and forth, and they spoke loudly and boldly in Spanish.

"You sick bastards," Peck whispered. The noise of the motors made it easier for him to speak.

I sat quiet for a minute. Peck shook his head and looked at me. He listened intently, as if he could understand the words.

"Half of this shit is for a 14-year-old at the middle school to sell." I just stared at him. He shook his head again. "I'm gonna kill every single one of these fucks," he said.

In no time, the engines were finally roaring. The boat was leaping up and down, zooming across the water, banging my head all over the place. "Are you ready?" Peck asked, holding up his gun.

"Yes!" I said. I just wanted to get the hell out of this space.

"Okay! Let's go!"

We maneuvered around the heavy blocks of drugs and scrambled up the steps as quickly as possible. My heart was pumping hard. When we reached the deck, the bright sun blinded us again, and burning ocean spray hit us in the face. It was loud as hell, and every single man on-board was turned away from us. There were four of them, and they were completely oblivious to the madman behind them.

The Pirate was up front, at the wheel, his black hair flowing. Peck fired and hit him squarely in the back of the head. His brains and blood blew back on both of us. Peck kept firing, but it was chaos. His first shot was lucky. The boat sped so fast, jumping up and down, that Pecks subsequent shots were all over the place. I don't know how many bullets were in his clip, but he remained calm and steady, firing away.

One of the men on-board spun around with a machine gun. He pulled the trigger and it was wide open. Peck hit the deck and I jumped back into the cargo hold. FUCK THIS.

I heard Peck continue. POW! POW! POW! POW! The buzz of the machine gun spanned wildly back and forth. I could hear bullets zinging in all directions.

POW! POW! POW! Then the machine gun stopped.

"Bill!" Peck screamed. "They're dead! Are you okay?"

I slipped and banged my way back up to the deck. Sure enough, everyone was dead. Bright red blood was everywhere, blowing back in cosmic airbrushed streaks across the white interior. Peck and I looked like drunks, stumbling from side to side of this unmanned vessel, throttle wide open. Peck made his way to the controls.

"FUCK. They're all shot up!" he screamed over the wind. He fumbled with them for a bit to no avail. Up ahead, an orange warning pole jutted from the sea.

"FUCK!" he shouted. "Jump now! Jump! Jump now!"

We both launched from the boat. When I hit the water, it felt like concrete. I heard a crunch and thought my jaw had broken upon impact.

When I came back up, gasping for air, I saw the boat hit the reef. It must've flown twenty feet into the air and crashed back down in an explosion, end over end, skipping across the water into the distance. I gulped salt water. OH FUCK. I felt like I was going to die. Suddenly, I was under water again, then back up, then under again, the shock wave of the crash attacking me in spurts. PLEASE JESUS, DON'T LET ME DIE.

Each time I surfaced, I saw the beach in the distance. Swimming technique was gone. I was now like a dog, fighting my way to the shore, drowning. Waves of saltwater kept slapping me in the face. My mind kept praying, begging to live. My arms and legs moved water behind me. Over and over and over until every muscle burned. I could no longer see. I just kept pushing and pushing. The sea kept pulling me back, but I would not accept this death.

Once in a while, I could see the beach as a blurry white line that was coming closer. I continued swallowing water, then sucking air, until, by the grace of Jesus, my feet touched a slimy bottom. I raced forward, shoving my 200 pounds ever closer to salvation. Finally, I was on the sandy shore, coughing up water. Saved.

I coughed and coughed and coughed. That's when I realized Peck was beside me. He had made it, as well. We both laid there on the beach coughing, feet rushing past us as people from the shore scrambled into the water for more survivors. It was a blur. I could finally breathe normally, though my heart seemed it would rip and pound from my chest. I looked over at Peck. He was up on his hands and knees like a dog, then he collapsed even closer beside me. We both laid there for a long time.

Finally, Peck stood up, grabbed my hands and pulled me up on wobbly legs.

"Are you okay amigo?"

"Yeah! Yes!" I said. "I think I'm okay."

Peck embraced me. It was a blessing to feel anything. He patted me on the back. We pulled apart. Peck put his hands on his knees and continued breathing deep. We just stood next to each other, happy to be alive for a few minutes, until our breathing reached a normal level. We brushed off all the onlookers asking us if we were alright. Then Peck looked up at the shore. He scanned the area. Suddenly his eyebrows popped up and a child-like smile flashed.

"Oh look," he said, pointing. "Pinchos!"

Peck trudged through the sand toward the Boqueron poblado. Pinchos?

I followed him as he headed straight toward a street

vendor by a rickety little stand. The vendor was a short, deeply-tanned man, soft and pudgy. He looked like a big 12-year-old with a well-manicured mustache. He stared at us like he was watching ghosts emerge from the deep.

Peck's hat hung behind his head from the neck-strap, and his sunglasses were still intact. He pulled his hat back up on his head.

"Two pollo pinchos senor," he said.

"Two pollo pinchos?" the vendor said.

"Si," Peck replied.

The vendor quickly retrieved two sharp, wooden skewers lined with juicy chicken meat and slathered with barbeque sauce. He impaled a couple pieces of fluffy, buttery, French bread on the ends.

"Es four dollar," he said.

Peck fished around then handed the man a five dollar bill.

"Eeeew," said the vendor, scrunching his nose as if he'd been tricked into grabbing a moist turd. "Es damp."

"It's all good, amigo," Peck assured him. "Just a little wet."

The vendor handed each of us a pincho. I almost killed myself shoving the pointed end in my mouth to gnaw off the meat and bread. It was the best thing I had ever tasted.

Peck brought out his cell phone and dialed. "Roberto!" he said. "It's Peck! I'm in the poblado. We need to get the fuck outta here right now!"

Was this real, or just a dream?

4

The Garadiablo

"That was like a movie, huh amigo?" Peck chuckled as we blew down the highway. I felt numb.

"Yep," I said.

"Man, I never saw anything like the way that boat flew up into the fucking air. That was awesome!" Peck continued to muse.

"Yep." I was completely zoned out.

"But don't you worry, amigo, we're gonna relax for a while now."

He pointed to the right side of the road. A large sign said "Laguna Cartagena—National Wildlife Refuge." We blazed on by. "That's the UFO Lagoon," Peck stated. "They see UFOs and USOs there all the time. In 1987 a big UFO crashed there and little aliens were running all over this place, in people's backyards, scaring the shit out of them." My mind was so dull and tired that I didn't even care what he was talking about.

"And look," he pointed to the right as we swung left at a fork in the road. "That's Route 303—the Extraterrestrial Highway. They call it that because so many people see

UFOs here. There's even an official sign on the side of the road. You want your picture beside it?"

"No," I said. I felt no emotion.

"Okay," Peck accepted my mental state. "You just kick back and relax then amigo." He turned on the car stereo, and Gnossienne No. 4 by Erik Satie, a soft, haunting piano piece, began to play. I closed my eyes and the sun beamed down warmly. Soon I was asleep.

✳ ✳ ✳

Sirens jarred me awake. I bolted upright in terror and confusion. Our car was parked on the side of a scenic little street. There was an old building with balconies beside us. "Where are we?"

"This is Ponce" Peck said. The siren was from a passing police car. I sighed.

"We're staying in a nice hotel here tonight."

"Is everything okay?" I asked. My brain still was not clear.

"Yes amigo. Everything is fine. You just relax. I'm gonna go inside and get us some rooms." He walked off. I looked around, squinting in the sun. It was a busy little town with a good deal of traffic and people walking by on the street. I leaned back and quickly drifted to sleep again.

The next thing I remember was being nudged on the shoulder. My eyes popped open to a scary face looming over me. I lashed out, but the face drew back.

"I'm sorry! I'm sorry!" It was just a vagabond, dirty and gnarled, with missing teeth and bloodshot eyes.

"I'm sorry, senor! Can you help me please?"

His hand was out. It was grossly swollen. He kept talking, but it was hard to understand his jumbled words. I just kept shaking my head "no," shooing him away from the car. Right as the bum turned to walk off, he bumped into Peck. The vagabond continued his pleas. Peck was holding room keys. He put them in his pocket and took out a couple dollar bills.

"Why sure amigo," Peck smiled. "But let me ask you somethin'. Where can I find a cockfight around here?"

* * *

The room Peck got me was simple and old, but nice. My eyes fell on the big cushy bed and it looked like heaven. I cranked up the air conditioner.

"I might sleep for days," I told him.

"Well listen, amigo," he said. "I got the rooms for two nights so we can sleep late tomorrow if we want. Before we go to sleep—and trust me, I'm gonna be out like a log, too—there's a nice restaurant downstairs. Do you wanna have a decent meal?"

Until he said that, I'd forgotten that I was famished.

"Yeah—that's a good idea," I said. "Lemmie take a shower and meet you down there in 30 minutes."

"Sounds good," he replied. "I'm in room 454."

* * *

Forty-five minutes later, quite refreshed, Peck and I entered the posh restaurant downstairs. Everything was white, kind of sterile really, but a candle burned on each square table. We were the only ones there. It was uncomfortably silent as the host seated us in the middle of the room. Soon a waiter took our drink orders, and Peck asked if we could have some music. I expected something tropical; instead a soft Britney Spears tune soon played in the background. It was weird to sit across from Peck, a candle flame wavering between us, in a lavish room. I was engrossed in my cell phone as Peck furrowed his brow, examining the extensive menu.

"I didn't know your mom was sick," Peck said.

"Oh really," my eyes stayed trained on my phone's screen. "That wasn't in your extensive file?"

The waiter came back with our drinks. I just ordered a club soda with lime. A fruity little strawberry concoction was placed in front of Peck. I asked for interpretation of the Spanish dishes on the menu, then we ordered our food. The waiter nodded and walked away. I was still looking at my phone instead of Peck.

"How is she doing?" Peck asked.

"She's going into surgery," I replied.

"Aren't you afraid the cops can trace you when you use that thing?" Peck asked, genuine concern in his voice.

"What difference does it make now?" I looked him in the eye.

For the first time, I saw a brief, blank look in his eyes, then he sipped his beverage.

"Let me ask you a question, amigo," he said.

"Yeah."

"Do you know about the power of belief?"

"What do you mean?" I laid my phone aside.

"Many years ago, I read this great book by Claude M. Bristol called The Magic of Believing," he sounded like a college instructor. "And," he hesitated, looking up into space for a moment, "the book is about how you can make anything happen if you believe it enough. It's about how the whole world is a flexible dimension, and when you truly believe something—if you use positive thinking—you can change it. That's what prayer is about. You should read that book, amigo. You might be able to help your mom."

"Okay," I said.

"I mean, think about it amigo," he continued. "Right now if you want to lift up your arm, you just think to yourself 'I want to lift up my arm,' and voila, you lift up your arm amigo." His right arm shot up and he knocked his spoon off the table. But Peck ignored it; nothing would stand in the way of his point. "Your mind controls your matter dude. And it extends beyond your body. If you believe something strongly enough, your mind makes it real for you."

"Oh really?" I said, snide and skeptical, at best. "Then what is real? 'Cause if everyone is believing something different, how do we know what is real?"

Peck picked up his spoon. As he wiped it with his napkin, he said "You make a very good point, amigo, and I'm glad you asked it." He placed the spoon neatly back on the table. "There was once a great Zen master whose student asked him, 'What is real, dude?' And the great master said 'What is real is that which never changes.'" Peck placed his hands together and bowed.

"That which never changes," I said sipping my club soda.

"Yeah man. Do you realize what that means?"

"What?"

"Everything changes," Peck pointed his finger at me. "So nothing is real. And if nothing is real, that means you can change it, my friend. You can fucking change it with your mind."

I thought about his words for a long time. The food came. It was an amazing feast. I don't think I said a single word during dinner, but Peck was happy to entertain me with philosophical musings, as usual.

"You know," he said, "I read something really weird in a book a long time ago. I can't remember who wrote it. I might have been Brad Steiger. Anyway, back in the 1920s, somebody in Nevada discovered a rock with a petrified shoe print in it. I mean this was an ancient rock, and the print had to be made millions of years ago. I've seen pictures of it, and it's fucking amazing. So do you know what that means, amigo? It means that either people existed way back then, long before they supposedly evolved. Or it means that we were visited by aliens or inter-dimensional beings way back then. Or it means that humans from the future traveled back to the past and walked around, same as we did on the moon. Personally, that's what I think happened. This is mainly because of freedom versus determinism and the Paratemporal Loop Hypothesis. Basically, we have to look at the nature of time itself. What separates the past from the future? This thing called the present. However, there is a little problem. No one can come up with a meaningful definition of what the present is. I mean, if the present lasts a second, a second still has a beginning and an end. That would mean there is a past and present within our past and present, and that simply does not make sense. In fact, there is no measurement for the present we can imagine that does not include its own little past and future. Therefore, the present is not real. And if the present is not real, that means the past and future are the same. They are only separated by our individual perceptions as we struggle to perceive the timeline all at once, but are incapable of doing so. And our own perception of living life and gliding along the timeline is what we perceive as time. So if, ever in the infinite future, creatures will someday learn to travel back in time, the Paratemporal Loop Hypothesis assumes that they will do it, and that we are living in a world that shifts, from day to day, moment to moment, as these beings are constantly coming back and fucking with things. That's why some of the men in black are around. These guys are like policemen trying to guard the timeline and keep some law and order in the wild west."

I was so tired I can barely remember much past that. I ate like a pig and then raced to bed in my historic room. I kind of remember falling in, and the sound of a large, old "crack," as I hit the unsteady bed. I knew that pillow would be drenched with slobber.

＊ ＊ ＊

The next morning, I woke up early. Pure, golden rays of sun gently lit my room. I slowly sat up, rubbed my eyes, and stood with a smile. I remembered I was in Puerto Rico.

We hadn't planned to meet downstairs, but we did, around 8am. Peck was at the restaurant bar, sipping coffee and trying to read a Spanish newspaper. The coffee smelled rich and great. I plopped down on the stool beside him. There was a nice, warm breeze blowing through the place.

"Buenos dias, amigo," Peck smiled. He seemed as alert and lively as ever.

"Morning," I replied.

"This is good Puerto Rican coffee," Peck said. He was wearing his hat and sunglasses, as usual. I looked at him like a caricature.

"Why are you always hiding behind your hat and sunglasses?" I asked.

"Are you kidding?" Peck raised his mug. "I'm pale amigo. I'm like a vampire. It's all too bright for me. I'm from North Carolina."

"Would you care for a cup of Café Rico?" he lifted his mug.

"Sure. Thanks."

"Okay, I'll order you one."

"Do they have laundry here?" I asked.

"Yes they do, downstairs."

"Good."

"SO, we have another big day here."

I was afraid he was going to say that. "How many more guys do we have to take out?" I asked with dread.

"Well, after this guy just two more," he said with great ease.

"So three more people?"

"Yeah, unless they give in before that. And if they're smart, they will, and they'll release our friend from outer space."

"And how will you know if they give in?"

"Numbers will contact me, man," he sipped his coffee.

"And how will they contact you?"

"They've got bugs all over my ass. Believe me, I will know."

"Of course," I stated rhetorically.

"How is your mom, amigo?"

"I don't know yet."

"Okay. Well let me tell you about our day."

"Who is the bad guy this time?" I asked.

He leaned close to me and whispered. "The Garadiablo."

"The what?"

"Garadiablo," he repeated. "G-A-R-A-Diablo, like devil."

"What the fuck is that?"

"Well," he became thoughtful, "there is a legend here, on the island, about a little gargoyle-looking bastard that runs around. He's just another one of the weirdies here that slips in and out through the portal. And some guy in the mountains named it 'Garadiablo.' I think it means something like 'gargoyle devil.'" Peck was about to continue, but then I realized he was suddenly distracted by a stray thought. "Hey amigo, you know I just thought about something that I haven't thought about in years."

"Uh huh," I said.

"Well a long time ago there used to be this television show I used to watch with Leonard Nimoy called In Search Of. Have you ever heard of that?"

"Uhh . . . I think so." It sounded familiar.

"So my wife knew how into this show I was and she would buy me books about unsolved mysteries and strange things. Reader's Digest had some good ones. And somewhere I remember reading about something bizarre that happened somewhere in Europe—I think it was France—in the 1800s. These guys were working on building a railroad or something, and they were using explosives to blow out these huge chunks of rock. So they set off a charge that opens up a little pocket of rock and—holy shit—lo and behold a creature comes staggering out. It was a big, winged thing with a beaked face and black, oily, leathery skin, and it just stumbled out and squawked or something, and then died right at their feet. It was obviously a fucking pterodactyl that had somehow been alive in this rock for maybe millions of years. I don't remember what happened to it. I think that may be another little conspiracy actually. All throughout history whenever people discover something weird like giant skeletons of humans with horns, or multiple rows of teeth or whatever, there are these big splashy headlines, and then all of a sudden some shadowy group closes in, like the Smithsonian, and—voila—the shit is never seen again. But, as a side note, I have always felt there's a good reason for it. I mean a good chunk of the Smithsonian budget comes from private contributions. So let's say you're a billionaire—I mean a real billionaire—like Bill Gates or somebody, and you go to the Smithsonian and say, 'guys, I'm gonna write you a fuckin' check for one billion dollars, but it's contingent upon one thing. Whenever you guys find somethin' cool, and I mean really cool, I get to see it first. And maybe, just maybe, I get to keep it in my own little collection for a while. So you have these super-rich guys out there who invite you over to their house for a nice dinner of bald eagle and bottle-nosed dolphin, and while you're enjoying a brandy digestif and Cuban cigar, they take you down to their collection of mounted sas-quatches, yeti, Nessie, and so on. It makes perfect sense to me that these fucking bastards would control all those grand specimens." Peck shook his head with disgust, and I was amazed at how he'd strung so many thoughts together in one long, bizarre stream of consciousness.

"Anyway, amgio," Peck snapped back. "Maybe that's what the Garadiablo is: one of these creatures from the past that somehow became trapped here, in these volcanic pockets, and was released again. So that's the name the dealer in this region uses. He has a tattoo of the thing on his arm."

"Okay," I nodded, and repeated the word: "Garadiablo."

"But here's the scoop on the real guy we gotta get." Peck looked very serious. "This motherfucker belongs in a cage," Peck dwelled gloomily. "He's big, strong, and likes to go on bath salt binges and eat your fucking face off."

"Oh Jesus." I sat back and crossed my arms.

"We're gonna find him today," Peck said confidently.

"I say we just sit on a balcony and snipe him. Doesn't that sound like a good idea?" I added helpfully.

"Maybe," Peck agreed. "But we have to be sure. If I kill an innocent person, I'm in big trouble."

"So I gather we're going to a cockfight?" I inquired.

"How did you know that, amigo?"

"Because you asked the bum yesterday."

"Oh. Yeah. Anyway," he said, "this guy likes to gamble on roosters. So we're gonna go to a cockfight, hopefully find him there, and take him out quickly. Maybe we'll even get lucky and make some money," he chuckled.

"All right," I said. "And you owe me some money, by the way."

* * *

That afternoon we pulled into the dusty, gravel parking lot of a giant barn. There must have been 100 or more cars crammed into the lot, pointed in all directions, forming a disjointed, metal maze.

"Cockfighting is legal here," Peck said as he slowly and carefully parked between two cars. "But this place is an illegal spot. Garadiablo takes a cut of everything."

I had been to illegal cockfights in Tennessee, so this scenario didn't seem too out of place to me. In Tennessee, even the local deputies used to hang out and monitor the underground activity. Peck and I ambled across the lot to the entrance. We were greeted by a little old Puerto Rican man wearing a ball cap. He looked at us with surprise.

"Cuanto?" Peck asked.

The man held up eight fingers. "Ocho," he said. He was missing most of his teeth.

Peck paid and we walked through a small, stinky corridor. The roars inside swelled with each step. We emerged on the edge of an amazing Romanesque arena, squirming with chaos and explosive energy.

I scanned the huge crowd. We were, by far, the only gringos. In fact, we looked like nerdy tourists compared to these men. They formed all classes—from dirty farmers to well-dressed businessmen. But they were all very comfortable Puerto Ricans, sharing a mammoth wave of enthusiastic violence. In fact, we looked so outstanding, I'm sure the entire crowd would have turned to look at us, perplexed, if they weren't so engrossed in the cosmic battles taking place on the stage.

There's no need to describe a chicken fight for you. You've surely seen the videos. Feathers were flying and fists were pounding the air. Peck and I took a seat in the back and relaxed. I knew he was looking for the Garadiablo. To me, it was all just madness most of the time. Once in a while, I could hear a consensus in the crowd—a collective cheer or sigh of disappointment. But most of the time, it was just loud noise and a million Spanish words per second.

Peck leaned over. "I think that's him," he said.

The fighting stage was a green circle down below. The men on the edge were obviously those with the most vested interests.

"Which one?" I asked.

"The one with the sunglasses," Peck replied.

When he said that, sure enough, I realized that, in this soaring room, filled with focused people, only one guy was wearing sunglasses. Not surprisingly, he also looked like the one guy in the building who could easily kick your ass.

The Garadiablo appeared to be in his mid-30s. He was a tall Puerto Rican with thick muscles. The guy was actually built like a wrestler. He had a shaved head and pock-marked face. His sunglasses were big, like a skier might wear, and they reflected the light like the eyes of a fly. He wore a skin-tight, short-sleeved shirt, and nice black pants with a white belt. His watch was bulky and bejeweled, just like the bracelet on his other hand. The gold and diamond rings on his fingers had surely been impressed, with a punch, on a thousand faces. He obviously enjoyed his bling.

"Keep your hands in your pockets," Peck said.

"Huh?"

"Do not move your hands or you'll end up betting $2000 on one of these chickens," Peck whispered.

"Oh, okay." I stuffed my hands into my pockets.

Garadiablo was shouting. There was something about the current fight he didn't like. He was soon jumping up and down, stamping his feet. I examined his large frame and bulging muscles. Then I leaned over to Peck.

"We should just sit in the dark and shoot this fucker from a distance," I said.

Peck noddeed. "I think you're right amigo. We just have to find out where he'll be. Hey look!" he pointed.

Down next to the stage, off to the side, was a short, pudgy, deeply-tanned man, with a well-manicured mustache. Why did he look so familiar?

"It's the pincho guy in Boqueron," Peck looked delighted. Then his expression changed. "Oh man. You don't think this is where he gets the chickens, do you?"

"Oh," it dawned on me. "Yeah, I bet you're right."

The fight was just ending with a flurry of blood. One chicken was now flopping around in choppy spurts of impending death.

"Si!!!" roared the Garadiablo, his fists clenched in glory. "Si!!!!!"

"I'll be right back," Peck said, rising and stumbling down the bleachers, through the excited crowd. I felt very alone in the midst of this madness.

My view was obscured by fistfuls of cash briskly trading all around me, yet I could see Peck had made it down to the pincho guy. In moments, they appeared to be greeting each other like old friends. Across the stage, in the chatter of the crowd, Garadiablo was collecting big winnings. He didn't even seem to notice Peck engaged in warm banter with the pincho vendor nearby. The scene looked comical to me. Peck stood out like an awkward snowman, a beacon of gringo-ness, in this sea of Puerto Ricans. And yet, oddly enough, no one even seemed to notice him. I suppose their minds were consumed and clouded with emotions—greed, ecstasy, and loss. As soon as one cockfight ended, they eagerly prepared for the next one.

Sweaty shoulders bumped me back and forth in this hot arena as the men around me clamored to place their next bets. Eventually, I stood and walked back up to the top of the stands, stepping away from the claustrophobic mess. I'd lost sight of Peck now, but I was quick to pick up a cold Medalla, for a buck, from a passing vendor. I'd just finished downing the cerveza when Peck suddenly appeared again. He looked happy as hell.

"Good news amigo!" he exclaimed. "I put in an order for a bunch of pinchos tonight. Manuel - that's the pincho guy," he explained, "said we can meet him at Gara's hive tonight."

"What the fuck is that?" my concern was apparent.

"He's got a big illegal casino in a warehouse. They're gonna be gambling tonight, and that's when we make our move. Let's go."

It was getting dusky as we walked the streets of Ponce. It was a perfect, quaint Puerto Rican town. We ambled past the historic firehouse, painted blood-red with black stripes. It almost seemed made of ornate gingerbread, and reminded me of the witch's house of horrors from Hansel and Gretel.

Lively people strolled the streets, and merchants had stands all along the way, selling every kind of cheap necklace, bracelet and trinket you could imagine. Both sides of the street were lined with clothing shops. These shops advertised their wares with rows of identical female half-mannequins, only waist down, their shapely, plastic asses turned toward passersby, flaunting a spectrum of gaudy, skin-tight pants.

"I've never seen so many fake asses," I muttered to Peck.

"You haven't been to Hollywood," he chuckled.

"I mean," I continued harping, "every single store has a row of ass mannequins. What the fuck? This says something deep about this culture."

"Yeah, it's great isn't it amigo?" Peck replied with genuine delight.

"Oh Jesus," he whispered sternly, his demeanor instantly changing.

"What?"

"Just keep walking," he said, looking straight ahead and upping his pace.

We walked a couple more minutes before darting into a dingy bar with black windows. A handful of men sipped their beers at the small bar inside as music played. They shot a glance at us, then went back to their business. Peck and I sat at the corner of the bar, as usual.

"What the hell's going on?" I asked.

"You didn't see that guy, did you?"

"What guy?"

"The guy with the blazer who passed us on the street. The real tall white guy," Peck raised his hand.

I strained to remember. "Ummm," I reflected.

"Did you see his ears?" Peck leaned in.

"No, I don't . . ."

"He had tiny-ass little ears," Peck nodded confidently.

"No, I didn't notice," I confessed.

"Well the guy had little ears. You know what that means?"

I shook my head no.

"He's an agent for one of the others."

"What? You mean the drug dealers?" I asked.

"No," Peck replied. "One of the others."

"What others?"

Peck sighed. "I'm not really sure, amigo. But there are other agents who want to get the alien. He was probably a Russian working with the Chinese."

"So, why little ears?"

"They all have tiny-ass little ears," he said. "And some don't even have any ears at all."

"Why?"

"Well," Peck speculated, "I think they've been playing around with reptilian genes. I mean that guy could have been a fucking alien wearing human skin, but for some reason, they can never get the ears right."

"Why would that be a problem?" I puzzled.

"I'm not sure amigo, but think about it. Whenever you hear stories about them fucking around with genes, and making new body parts, they're always growing ears. You remember the mouse with an ear on its back?"

"Yeah," I said. "I remember something about that."

"Well I saw it on TV," Peck said. "They grew an ear on a mouse's back. They're trying to create a farm for body parts, and they always start with the ears. Why? Because they need ears, that's why. At least that's my theory."

The bartender, a dusky guy, took our drink orders.

"So you're saying there is a conspiracy between the

Russians and Chinese to make Reptilian agents in human skin to get this alien creature the drug dealers are keeping hostage?"

"Yeah, that's it, amigo," Peck sounded proud. "These reptilians have always been a pain in the fucking ass. I mean you've read the Bible. How does it start? It starts where Adam and Eve are happy little puppies living in the Garden of Eden. All is cool and then, one day, who shows up? A fucking reptilian. They usually show him as a snake in the movies, but the Bible describes him a little differently. I mean I don't know a fucking snake that can talk, do you? So he tempts everybody and screws up mankind and then reptiles are supposedly damned to slither on their bellies. So again, before this reptilians could apparently walk around. Well the ones that can still walk around are still out there.

"Oh, and I'll tell you something else weird," Peck rambled on, "Have you ever heard of the third eye?"

"Yes," I shook my head affirmatively.

"It's supposed to be a psychic eye that's somewhere on the forehead between the other two eyes. That's why Hindus wear a little red dot on their foreheads. It's supposed to represent the third eye that is still in the process of evolving in humans. And a lot of people who use psychic power, or are able to see auras and shit, are tapping into the view they can get through the third eye, shifting their consciousness upward. Well did you know that reptiles already have a fucking third eye? It's called a parietal eye or pineal eye. So do sharks, lampreys and other nasty little bastards. Coincidence? I think not, amigo. The reptilians have a one-up on us mammals, and if we're not careful, we warm-blooded souls are gonna be shred into cattle grain."

"My guys are not the only ones trying to free the good alien and protect all the secrets. Bigger problem is that the aliens keep fucking things up by visiting the humans on this island and telling them shit. I mean all these governments are here experimenting with alien genes and monkey genes and iguana genes and working on top-secret projects in underground bases. Yet the aliens keep talking to the spiritual people here and telling them what's going on. I'll explain more later, but this is not the place and time, amigo."

"Okay," I said, resolving to take one thing at a time. "So then what are we going to do tonight?"

"Oh, tonight will be easy," Peck waved his hand. "We're gonna go to Garadiablo's hive. And when the time is right I'm gonna shoot his ass and we run. I mean this guy's a fucking moron. It'll be easy. A lot easier than I thought it would be, now that I've seen his setup."

My beer arrived and I downed nearly all of it in one series of gulps. "So can I just stay in the room tonight and let you handle this shit?" I said.

Peck smiled. "I need you there to back me up amigo. You never know when something can fuck up."

✳   ✳   ✳

That night we weaved through some alleyways and found the warehouse, Garadiablo's "Hive," on the outskirts of downtown. Music was pumping inside, along with the dull roar of crowds, including an occasional yell. Frenetic shadows moved across the frosted windows. In the darkness, I couldn't tell much about the large building, but it seemed to be buried under layers of history—a wooden structure nestled firmly in broken-down outer walls of brick. I felt this place had been something off and on for hundreds of years and was now in a truly dismal phase.

As we walked toward the entrance, we encountered clouds of smoke from a dozen sloppy men chattering and puffing on cigarettes in the half-light. Once we reached the door, they all looked to us curiously. My skin crawled. Thank goodness, the next thing we saw was the beaming face of the pincho guy, happy as a clam to see us.

"Amgio!" his robust face smiled, clasping hands with Peck, and pulling into a brief hug.

"Manuel!" Peck returned the enthusiasm.

"So good to see you, my friend!" Manuel continued.

Man, I thought to myself, Peck must have ordered a fuckload of pinchos.

We were still getting strange looks from the guys outside, but any tension was greatly deflated once the pincho guy greeted us.

"This is Bill," he said, referring to me. For the first time,

I cringed a bit at Peck using my real name. Maybe we should have come up with fake names for this shit.

"Beel!" he called me. "Welcome my friend!"

I smiled, shaking his hand heartily. "Thank you, thank you."

"I have you pinchos," Manuel said. He turned and raced over to his cart. I hadn't even noticed it until then. The wonderful aroma of grilling meat had been hidden by all the cigarettes.

Manuel came back with a large plastic bag and plopped it into Peck's arms.

"Oh," Peck reacted. "They're hot."

"Of course! Of course, my friend," Manuel laughed. "They are good for you!"

Peck shifted the bag to his left arm and fished around in his pocket for cash.

"You going to have a good party tonight for you friends," Manuel assured him.

Peck handed him some bills and Manuel counted them briskly.

"Keep the change." Peck said. "So what kind of party is going on here tonight?" Peck referred to the Hive.

"Oh, lotsa fun, as usual. Dey are gambling and fighting and drinking. Is good time."

"We'd like to do some gambling tonight. I have mucho dinero burning a hole in my pocket."

"Oh, okay. Good!" Manuel replied. "You will be welcome then. Just go on inside."

"You sure?" Peck played coy.

"Of course, of course," Manuel seemed earnest. "Just go inside and have some fun."

"Okay; thanks amigo," Peck said. He looked at me and we walked through the tattered old door.

We stepped into a world bursting with energy. It was not as explosive as the cockfights, but more reckless and intense. There was shouting and laughter in the background, and we glimpsed flashes of action through the next doorway before us. This first room we stepped into was a kind of lobby, guarded by bouncers, and there were a couple guys waiting in line to get in before us. I realized the one up front was being frisked. I flashed a glance at Peck and saw the blank, "oh fuck" expression on his face. This was not good. My instinct was to simply turn and walk back out the door. Peck immediately sensed my feelings. He shot a giant, fake grin at me. "All is cool amigo," he said.

"All is cool."

The big guy doing most of the frisking was born to be a bouncer. He was bald and thick, wearing a white tank top, with a shrub of coal-black hair on his chin. And he was thorough. 100 percent of his attention was on the man he felt up, sliding his hands all over and squeezing hard. His two bouncer cohorts were just as absorbed in the task, double checking the crevices.

My heart was pounding in my chest. I wasn't armed, but I knew Peck was. He always was. And whenever Peck got into a crunch, his solution was to shoot his way out. I didn't expect it to start this early, though. This was gonna be bad.

They let the guy through. "Proximo," the bouncer said, and the next guy stepped up. I swear, they must have spent five minutes on him, asking him questions in Spanish and frisking him just as thoroughly. Please, I telepathically begged Peck, let's turn and leave!

Just as it was Peck's turn, Manuel stepped in. He smiled and said something to the bouncers in Spanish. All I understood was the word "amigos."

"Okay, okay," the bouncer replied. With an ever-stern face, he motioned for Peck to step up.

"Hasta," the bouncer said. Peck looked perplexed. "Up. Up!" the bouncer motioned. Peck placed down the pinchos and lifted his hands. They began frisking Peck. In just a few moments, the bouncer paused over his right leg. We could all see an object there. I held my breath. Peck looked so helpless, standing there in his dorky shirts with his thin, pale arms raised in the air.

"What's this?" the bouncer firmly jiggled the object.

Peck looked down—looked him right in the eye—and calmly said, "why that's my schlong, amigo. I'm not wearing any underwear."

All the guys laughed. It was the first time they'd so much as cracked a smile. But it would take more than a chuckle to end this peacefully. The bouncer ran his hand deep into Peck's right pocket and pulled out a metal can of bug spray. "Boqueron cologne," Peck winked. All the guys nodded in sympathy. After a few more thorough swipes, Peck was through. I couldn't believe it.

I was up next. And yes, they squeezed and prodded every inch of yours truly. Thankfully, I was clean as a whistle. Amazingly, Peck and I were soon through to the other side, watching our first taste of the real action.

We entered a rather small room with a group of men crowded around a heavy wooden table. It was an arm wrestling stage. Two Puerto Ricans, both in tank tops, veins and muscles bulging, were engaged in the middle of a painful bout. One guy was clearly much bigger than the other, and yet the small guy was holding his own. We watched them go back and forth until it looked like the small guy was getting the upper-hand. Then the big guy, spit flying from his strained lips, began cursing at the little man. It was apparently psychological warfare. And it was working. Suddenly, every man in the room erupted in a "OOOOH!!" at something that was said. The little guy, in a fit of rage, ripped back his hand and leapt across the table at his opponent. This arm wrestling match had become a fight.

We couldn't see much amidst the chaos. But soon enough, the two were pulled apart by other bouncers. I could gather they were told that brawling had to be conducted elsewhere, and so the party was moving into the next room.

"What happened?" I said, expecting Peck to answer.

Instead, a Puerto Rican man next to me shook his head seriously and said, "he called him a very bad name."

"What?" I asked.

"I don't even want to say it," he replied.

"What?" I implored. "Maybe I need to know this word?"

The man shook his head disdainfully. "He called him a cabrone."

"A cabrone?"

"Si. Cabrone."

"What does that mean?"

The man looked troubled just thinking about it. He closed his eyes. "It . . . it doesn't translate into English," he replied gravely, then walked off toward the new action.

I looked at Peck. "Cabrone?" Peck shrugged.

We moved into the next room. It was filled with noisy slot machines being played by old men. The two arm wrestlers were pounding the shit out of each other, and the bouncers kept trying to pull them apart. The bouncers were obviously getting pissed, although the roomful of spectators loved it. It seemed the bouncers were quickly dragging the men through that room into the next one. I could already see another, much more immense crowd, through the doorway ahead.

Peck and I followed the mob into the next room. Holy shit. It looked like the cockfighting arena, but there were two men fighting in this one. Both men were drenched in blood. The crowd around were pounding their fists like a scene from a bad Jean Claude Van Damme movie. I was engulfed in a swirling wave of barbaric anger, hate, and violence. There was no true law or order here. It was scary as hell.

The room was stifling hot, and reeked of sweat. Down at the edge of the arena, surrounded by henchmen, sat Garadiablo. He looked like a ruthless king on a brutal throne. He was still wearing his sunglasses, but now donned a tight, white t-shirt. Even from that distance, I could see sweat glistening on his large, round cranium. There were piles of cash all around him, and he was intensely watching the fight, then occasionally yelling at those nearby, spearing the air angrily with his powerful index finger.

Peck leaned over to whisper to me, but it was so loud, his whisper turned into a shout. "Here!" he shoved the bag of pinchos into my arms. "Wait here amigo! I'll be right back!"

Where the hell was he going? He raced down through the bleachers and over toward Garadiablo. Peck was quickly grabbed by the guards at the bottom. Had this guy completely lost it now? I watched him smile and wave his arms around in the most animated display, talking his way through something. What on earth was he saying to them? Peck's hand ran deep into his pocket. Oh shit. Did he smuggle in his gun? Was it going to happen now? He pulled out his wallet and filed through the cash, pulling out a nice little stack. One of the guards walked over and got the attention of Garadiablo—no easy task in the midst of this fight. Gara rose, walked over to Peck, lowered his glasses, and looked him in the eye. Soon, Gara turned and gazed up at me with shark-black eyes. I shuddered. He nodded. Peck motioned for me to come on down. This did not feel good.

I clumsily made my way down through the crowd, holding the bag of pinchos like a baby. When I was finally a few feet from Gara, I realized just how thick and massive this guy was. I don't think he was taller than me, just built like a solid block. I stood there sheepishly, and he took a close look at me. He and Peck spoke for a moment, the Gara nodded. My heart began to pound, and I telepathically cried to Peck "Don't be signing me up for anything you motherfucker."

There was some shaking of hands, but all I remember was a lot of confusion really. Next, I heard a wave of "BOOOO" rolling from the crowd. I looked to the fighting ring to see one bloody man flopping around on the floor, almost like he was having a seizure. His opponent, equally bloody, was still raging over him, screaming at him, daring him to arise and continue to fight. It was a pitiful sight.

"Momento," Gara raised his finger. He then waded over toward the ring.

Peck leaned over to me, smiling like hell. "I just put two thousand dollars on you, amigo. You're gonna fight this big bastard. This is awesome!"

"No, I'm not", I said. I was pissed now. "No I'm not. Fuck you."

"It's part of the plan, amigo," Peck said, his voice barely audible over the white noise of the crowd. Suddenly the sound of the crowd shifted.

I turned to see Gara in the fighting ring holding a common carpenter's hammer. He towered over the poor man flopping around on the dirt floor. The pitch of the crowd became more and more shrill as Gara raised the hammer and then pounded the man's skull a couple times. The man instantly stopped moving. I presumed he was now dead.

"FUCK THIS!" I screamed, throwing the bag of pinchos back to Peck. "This is bullshit! I'm leaving!"

"Don't worry amigo!" Peck smiled. "It's just for fun! I won't let anything happen to you. It's part of the plan!"

I'd had enough. I turned to tear my way back up through the crowd and outta there. But I was surprised when the henchmen grabbed me. Three or four of them, with strong arms, held me firmly. What the FUCK was happening? Sheer terror, like cold ice water, poured over my skin, and I saw Gara motion for me to be brought toward the ring. What the FUCK had Peck done to me?

Everything was a sweeping blur. The lights at the side of the ring blinded me. Soon Gara had a microphone in his hand. It squealed for a moment, then he spoke.

"Everyone!" his voice was deep and resonant. "Everyone; I am speaking in English so our gringo friends can understand." The crowd hushed. "You know," his voice resonated, and the crowd hushed more, "you know," he raised his finger, "this island, Puerto Rico, has always been a place of war. The Taino Indians fought with the Caribs--who were cannibals--and then the Spaniards came. And the Spaniards enslaved and worked the Tainos to death, and then the Spaniards brought over the black Africans and worked them to death. And then the English came and were defeated. And then the Dutch came, and were defeated. And then, in 1898, the Americans came, and they are just the latest invaders of our beautiful little island. And you know what, when the Americans came, in their green outfits, we said to them 'Green, GO!' And that is why we call these filthy white people gringos. But you see these two gringos right here? They are special. Because you may have heard that there are some coward gringos going around the island and shooting people in the back of the head and stealing their belongings. Well, I think this is them," the Gara swept his hand toward us. Even Peck looked surprised and outraged by the statement.

"I think this is Numbers," Gara continued. The crowed booed. "I think he is a murderer; a gringo maniac. And I don't know who this little cambrone is," he pointed at me, "but I'm sure he is a little coward, too."

Peck stood with a blank look on his face.

"Mister Numbers here," said Gara, "is a big man with his 9mm gun. But no one is armed in this room! Without weapons, let's see just how strong these cowards are in the ring with Garadiablo." Everyone cheered madly.

"I will tear them apart inch-by-inch with my bare hands and feed their shitty meat to my chickens. Let's show them what happens when you foolishly come to the Hive of the Garadiablo!"

The crowd cheered and I glanced over to Peck. He was mouthing something. I shook my head that I couldn't understand him. He mouthed some more.

"This guy is an ASSHOLE," he said.

They guards threw me into the ring. I landed on all fours, and immediately a rain of garbage was hurled at me from the crowd.

"No, no," said Gara through the microphone as he walked back off to the sidelines. "No need for that. Just let him sit and be scared for a little while like the little lizard he is."

In the middle of the ring, the heat of the lights blaring down on me, I was overcome by the most dire and hopeless terror I'd ever felt. I was disoriented and panicked. This was all wrong. I stood, my hands covered in sand clumped with dark blood. Off to the side, I saw Gara sitting back at his table and eagerly snorting a pile of white powder up his nostrils. He threw his head back in burning pain and ecstasy. Then he stood, pounded his chest like an ape, and jumped up and down shouting, kicking and roaring. The crowd loved it.

The next thing I knew, Gara was stomping into the ring, half-bull and half-Frankenstein, a hybrid of man, drugs, and madness. He tossed off his glasses and stared at me with eyes so black and deep that all light and gravity seemed to warp around them. He pointed his finger at me like the sword of the angel of death. "You!" he screamed, then shouted something in rambling Spanish.

"YOU will now die!"

With that, his hulking form charged at me with full speed. It was tunnel vision. Suddenly, all I could see was him, and all the rest was silent. I braced for the impact of his stampeding weight. But at the very last second something—my fighting nature—my survival instinct—my talent—kicked in. I side-stepped and tripped him. His magnificent formed plowed hard, face-first, into the dirt. I immediately leapt on his back and locked my arms around his thick throat from behind. I could sense the crowd on their feet, insane emotion ripping through the air around me. Now, I would choke him to death. Or so I thought.

He was the strongest beast I had ever held, and he was quickly up again, me hanging on his back like a tall child swinging side-to-side, and he leapt backward, falling on top of me. It knocked all the air from my chest. I struggled to keep working my grip into his throat as he groped at my hands, sweaty flesh slipping on sweaty flesh. Finally, he slung me off, and the crowd rejoiced.

Instantly, he was atop me, punching down and ramming his knees into me. I covered my face, waiting for a moment to slip free. I saw an opening and punched upward, cracking him good on the nose. But he pressed me back down, holding my arms at the side. And then his face was against mine. I was afraid he would head-butt me, so I struggled to hold him close to me. I've watched plenty of MMA fights, and they were nothing compared to this violent wrestle to the death.

He was frustrated that I would not give him leverage. I saw him raise his head and open his mouth. There were large, gleaming, monstrous teeth. The next thing I felt was the worst pain of my life. He sunk his teeth into my cheek. I screamed pitifully and shoved him with all my might. FUCK. I remembered. He was going to eat my fucking face off.

This is the point in the story when I truly felt all was over. A crazed horse of a man was ripping into me with his wild teeth, and there was nothing I could do. It was as horrible as you think it was. I closed my eyes and prayed. "PLEASE JESUS, HELP ME! PLEASE! I WILL NEVER SIN AGAIN!"

There I was, on my back, crushed, helpless, dying. From the side of my right eye, I saw Peck run into the ring. Everyone gasped. My eye was squooshed, and vision blurred, but I saw Peck raise the bag of pinchos high above his head and smash it, with incredible force, over Gara's head. Immediately, Gara withdrew and howled in pain. Barbeque sauce spilled everywhere. Gara reached back, clamoring to pull an array of sharp pincho sticks from the back of his head and ear. Desperately, I grabbed a handful of pinchos and shoved them hard into his eyes. I could feel some of them sink deep into his sockets. He screamed again, wiping in horror at his face. I grabbed another pincho and stabbed him in the face over and over, sticks breaking in my hand.

Only then, I noticed Peck on all fours, swiping through the mess of barbeque in the ring. The guards were on top of him, dragging him back. Just when it looked like they would pull him away, his hand found a lump of sauce. He dug deep, raised it and fired. It was his gun.

The guards quickly cleared. As Garadiablo howled in pain, still atop me, pinchos hanging from his eyes, Peck put the gun to Gara's head and fired again. The villain's head split in half, blood and brain spraying in with the barbeque sauce. The blast of the gun was deafening to me.

Peck pulled me out from under Gara's dead body, back up on my weary feet. Everyone in the room was clearing like cockroaches, their hair practically standing with fright.

"Let's go amigo!" he exclaimed.

The two of us raced back toward the front door. The men around us, once so gung-ho to see death, were now shoving themselves through the doorways, scraping and banging their heads and bodies to get out. When the two of us had almost reached the front door, there was one last defender of Garadiablo standing there. He was a tall, thin man wielding a broad machete. He held it up in front of us. This guy was obviously confused, since Peck held up his gun, yet the man would not back down. He kept rambling in Spanish.

"Move!" Peck shouted. "Detener amigo!"

But the tall man would not budge. He was clearly scared, backing and hunching away, yet insisting on guarding the door.

"Calm down," Peck said. "Calmarse, calmarse. Just move amigo. You need to chill the fuck out."

Men were running all around us to get out, but this guy was simply too disoriented to realize the exact situation. "MOVE!" Peck shouted.

The man still would not budge, so Peck shot him in the left kneecap and we blasted by him and out the door.

"Some of these guys are dumb as hell!" Peck proclaimed as we fled across the outside lot.

We stormed through the alleyways, finally leaping into the car and hauling ass. "Woo-hoo!" Peck rejoiced as we tore down the street, warm wind blasting us. I was still numb with adrenaline, afraid to even touch my face. It was just beginning to burn from the barbeque sauce. My right ear was still pulsating with rumbling deafness.

"Now THAT was kickass!" he laughed maniacally.

"I should kill you, motherfucker," I said, my blood boiling.

"What?"

"I said I should kill you, you piece of shit!" I roared in rage. "What was the fucking point of that!"

"Hey, hey, calm down pussy," Peck reprimanded me. "Don't forget what we're doing here."

"What ARE we doing here! I thought you were going

to do this shit undercover. And you send me to fight this bastard and kill him in front of everyone. What the fuck is the point!"

"Just calm down, amigo," his demeanor was stern. "I got a little carried away, but I knew you could take that piece of shit."

"I couldn't!" I screamed. "He bit my goddamn face!"

"But you were doing an amazing job, dude. You were kicking his ass."

"No I wasn't, dickhead! He was eating my fucking face!"

"Look," he said, "I apologize if you're pissed at me. But remember, I'm not your buddy here. You're helping me and I'm helping you, so have some respect."

"You're just fucking with me!" I returned.

"I needed to see," he calmly stated.

"See what?"

"I needed to see just how good you were. And I needed to make it clear to everyone who I am."

"And why the hell is that?"

"Because," he said. "I have got to get El Brujo. And I'll never find him. So I've got to make him want to find me."

"Who the fuck is El Brujo?"

"He's the main guy here. Look, I'll explain later. But for now, we've done a great job. And I'm gonna pay you two thousand dollars for that, and we're gonna spend a nice night in a nice place."

"Where are we going?"

"We're gonna go to my favorite place, amigo."

"But I need to go back to the room," I said.

"Huh?"

"I need to go back to our hotel room."

"Are you crazy?" he shook his head. "We can't go back. We gotta get the F-U-C-K outta dodge, amigo."

"No," I said.

He slammed on the brakes and almost swung my head off as we hit the grade on the side of the road.

"What the fuck are you talking about? We've got to go, amigo."

I spoke slowly and deliberately. "My cell phone is in the room, and I have to get it."

"You left your cell phone in the room?"

"Yes."

"Why?"

"'Cause I was afraid it might get stolen at that place."

Peck dropped his head and rubbed his eyes, defeated. "Goddamnit dude, are you serious?"

"Yes."

"Well fuck your phone!" he raised his voice.

"Listen to me, you son-of-a-bitch, that phone is the only link I have to find out how my mother is doing. I got my fucking face eaten tonight and I'm not leaving here without my goddamn phone!"

He could tell I had seriously had enough. We sat there a moment, and he continued rubbing his brow.

"Okay," he said. "Okay. But this could go really, really

badly. You understand that, don't you? We should be running away right now, not heading back into town."

"Yes," I said. "I understand. But this is the most important thing to me right now."

We sat there for a minute as he thought about things. "Okay," he said. "Okay."

Peck whipped the car around, and we zoomed off into the night, back toward Ponce. This was truly insane, but I knew it must be done.

The plaza of Ponce at night was beautiful. A lit fountain glowed in the middle, and smiling people meandered in the evening air. We found a spot right in front of the hotel, and Peck took his time with a perfect parallel park. I hopped out and a dog was barking at us from a balcony somewhere above. He probably smelled the barbeque sauce. We both looked like murder victims, spattered with brown and red. God only knows how my face looked.

"We gotta get in an out quick," Peck said. He stuffed his gun in his pants. "Damn, this thing is sticky," he said. "I hope it doesn't get gummed up."

We walked casually into the front lobby, pretending to be calm. As fate would have it, the lobby was empty and the front desk man, more of a teenager, soaked us in.

"Mios dios!" he exclaimed.

We both laughed fakely. "The pigeons are a bitch around here," Peck said.

We breezed by him and up the stairs.

"Let's make it quick," Peck said quietly.

We were both out of breath by the time we reached my room on the fourth floor. I fumbled with my keys. This hotel was old-fashioned—just a good ol' lock and key. Right as I brought the key toward the lock, Peck grabbed my hand. I looked to him and saw him draw his finger to his lips.

"Shhhh," barely escaped his lips.

"What?"

"Did you leave the light on?"

"No."

"Look," he pointed down. I saw a crack of light coming from the bottom of my door. We locked eyes. Peck motioned for me to step back down the hallway a ways.

"You think someone is in there?" I said.

"Let's just watch for a minute," he replied.

We stood for a bit, and eventually saw shadows slip back and forth in the crack of light. Shit, I thought to myself.

"Let's just go," Peck whispered.

"No," I said firmly. "My fucking phone is in there."

"Well if you walk in there, someone is probably gonna kill you," he explained calmly.

I closed my eyes and took a deep breath, thinking for a moment. "What can we do?"

"Are you sure you wanna do this?" Peck asked.

"Yes. I have to have my phone. I can't just get another one so easily. I'm a fugitive."

Peck shook his head with acceptance. "All right," he

said. "You can't go in there, 'cause that's what they want. So we have to bring them out."

"And how do we do that?"

"Tell you what," he said. "I'll find the switchbox and turn the lights out on this floor. Chances are they'll come out. When they do, I'll turn the lights back on. You'll have just a second to take 'em out and get your phone."

"How should I take 'em out?"

"Just punch 'em in the face fast and hard, amigo. Or punch 'em in the stomach so they can't make a sound. You know the drill."

"Okay," I replied, butterflies fluttering in my stomach again, "okay."

"Are you ready?"

"Yeah," I said. "Sure."

Peck crept off down the hallway. I seemed to wait forever. He came back and said:

"Okay—I found it. Get right outside the door and get ready amigo. You can't hesitate. You have to do this quickly or bad shit will happen to you."

"Yeah, yeah, I got it," I said.

"Keep your eyes closed until I turn the lights back on," he explained, "so you'll have your night vision. When I turn the lights on, they'll be a little bit blinded and you'll have the advantage." This actually didn't make a lot of sense.

"What's the fucking difference?" I asked.

My question didn't matter. Peck crept back away as I walked over next to my hotel door. I thought about how fucking hot I'd been all day, and how steaming hot it was now. I wiped sweat from my brow. It was now so sticky that it felt like glue had been smeared above my eyes.

Click. The lights were gone. It was cave-black. I mean it was as black as you can imagine. My eyes could not detect one photon of light, then I closed them. I heard a voice behind the door of my room say something in another language. Then another man's voice replied. I balled my fists and prepared. Sure enough, in less than a minute, the door opened. Apparently Peck was in a position to hear it, because he instantly turned the lights back on.

I opened my eyes. I'll never forget that one millisecond in time. Before me was a 6-foot man in a dark suit, white skin, cropped blonde hair, rectangular head. His nose was square, his mouth was square, and his eyes were square. You could have drawn this guy with a ruler. His eyes were tiny and so blue they almost looked white. His pupils were in a state of disarray, filled with surprised panic, when he saw me. I had a split-second to make a decision, and I couldn't imagine that hitting him in his blockhead would do any good. So I drew back and socked him as hard as I could in the gut, curving my hand up into his vital organs. I actually felt a wave of cold air expel his lungs and hit me in the face. It smelled like he'd been eating onions. His eyes squinted and he fell backward, devoid of life-giving breath. That was no problem. But who was behind him?

He fell backward. The guy behind him looked almost identical. I was stunned by this, but without hesitation, punched that fella the same way. Now they were both on the ground, wallowing and gasping. I kicked by them into the room and realized they had pistols. Peck was right on top of them.

"Get your phone!" he ordered in a low tone.

Peck was holding his gun right on them. I swiped my phone and charger from a small table near the window. Peck stared down on them intensely. He couldn't resist the opportunity.

"Who are you?" he grabbed the first man by the lapel and slammed him back and forth a bit. The man had no breath to answer. Then Peck shoved the man's face over to the right side. "Look!" he called to me. I rushed over. "Look!" Peck stressed again. "Tiny fucking ears!"

Sure enough, that guy had the smallest ears I had ever seen. He barely had ears at all. Then Peck turned his attention to the second man. I could see the two men were not actually identical, but pretty damn close in appearance.

"Look at his ears!" Peck marveled. "TINY FUCKING EARS."

"You bastards," Peck said. He had now taken both of their guns. "Who are you?"

The first man was just now gaining enough breath to force out a raspy response. He said something in a language I could not understand. And yet Peck seemed to understand it, and whatever the man said seemed to disgust Peck.

"Suck my dick, you piece of shit," Peck replied. He then

karate-chopped each of the men in the throat. I cringed in horror, hearing their windpipes break, and watching their eyes roll back into their heads as they began to die.

"Let's go," Peck said.

I began to run down the stairs. "Calm!" exclaimed, and I held back. "Walk down slowly."

We slowly, naturally mozied down and back through the lobby. "Buenas noches," Peck tipped his hat to the front desk man.

We jumped back into the car and pulled out. As we zoomed around the blocks to escape town, each red light seemed to last forever. Soon enough, we were on back roads again, and Peck was gunning it down each stretch and around every curve.

"What did that guy say to you?" I asked.

"Ahh, he was just telling me to go fuck myself in so many words."

"What language was that? Russian?"

"Yeah."

"How do you know how to speak Russian?"

"I'm an agent, amigo. I know a little bit of everything about these bastards. You just kick back and relax now."

I leaned back and enjoyed the Puerto Rican breeze in my hair. In no time, I was asleep.

✳ ✳ ✳

When I opened my eyes, we were still. I could hear the tiny coqui frogs chirping. I looked over to see a campfire burning. The tent was already set up, and were pulled off into the woods again.

"Damn, how long was I out?"

"Ever since we left Ponce," Peck said. He looked clean. "But all is good now, amigo."

I barely pulled my weary body out of the car, and my legs were wobbly.

"I'm glad you got some rest amigo," Peck said kindly, stoking the fire.

"Where are we?"

"We're near Guanica," he replied.

"Where the fuck is that?"

"We're in the south, near the dry forest."

I still didn't know where we were, but I took a piss and stumbled over to sit down beside the fire. "I need a bath," I said.

"We're right next to the water. Just go take a dip. That's what I did."

"Is it salt water?"

"Yep."

"It's gonna burn then."

"Yeah, but it'll heal you, amigo. These are the healing waters that Ponce De Leon was looking for. The fountain of youth. Do you know why he was looking for it?"

"Why?"

"Because he couldn't get his dick hard. He was looking

for the fountain of Viagra. And guess where they make Viagra now." I shot him a skeptical look. "That's right amigo; right here in Puerto Rico."

"Oh, this is gonna suck," I said as I rose and ambled toward the edge of the dark water.

"Just take the plunge amigo," Peck inspired me, "you'll feel like a million bucks on the other side."

I waded into the water. It felt cold at first, then I lurched in and splashed around. Holy shit, my face burned. And a few other places burned, as well. When I dragged out of the water, I somehow felt ten pounds lighter.

"Here. Dry off by the fire, amigo," Peck said. He had pork and beans sizzling in a pot. I plopped down on a log next to the fire.

"You know," I said, "I feel like I'm just constantly fucked up. And I want out. Even if I have to go prison, I can't be a part of this anymore. I need to go."

Peck didn't say anything for a while. "How's your mom?"

"She's doin' okay," I nodded. "But that's part of what I'm saying. I think I should just turn myself into you, or whatever law enforcement, and go pay my dues, do my time, and get my life back on track. I think that's the smart thing to do. I don't want to get wrapped up in the stuff you're doin. You're doing things that are far, far worse than anything I've ever been exposed to. I'd never seen anyone get killed until I met you. I'm not cut out for this shit."

Peck sighed. His hat was off, and he stoked the fire

some more. "I'm glad your mom is okay. Remember, my friend, if you believe something strongly enough, you can make it happen." His face shifted somewhat, and looked pained. "I wanna tell you somethin' amigo," he said.

"Okay."

Peck leaned back and gazed up at the stars dotting the heavens. "I've been doin' this beat for a long time. I've been comin' to this island for years. And one of the things that intrigued me early on were these cases that were affecting people all across the mainland. Weird, weird, magical stuff, amigo. It took many, various forms, amigo, but here is how it usually worked out." Peck leaned forward. "I kept hearing the same kind of story from different, separate people, all across the island. A couple would go to bed, and in the middle of the night, they would wake up to see a glowing ball of white light hovering at the foot of the bed. They were petrified with fear. And then the ball of light would make a noise. To one person, usually the woman, it would just sound like a tape recorder sped up in fast motion." He made a sound with his mouth like the squiggly tones of a high pitched dolphin. "You know what I mean?"

"Yeah."

"But to the other person, usually the man, the noise sounded different. It sounded like a calm, fatherly voice. And it always said the same thing. It said," he made his voice sound resonant, "'Do not be afraid. Something big is about to happen on this island, but you will be okay.' Then, the light would go POP, and disappear as sparks flew all over the place. Pretty wild, huh?"

"Yeah," I said, helplessly mesmerized by his voice and the firelight.

"For years, I wondered what this meant," Peck continued, "until last year. Last year, something happened to me. I went to Mayaguez one night and picked up this voluptuous little brunette woman at a club. What a sweet, perfect face and ass and legs and tits. She invited me back to her house. She lived right next to the water. We made such sweet love that night. OH," he closed his eyes and reminisced. "We had wine, I could hear the waves crashing outside, the wind chimes were banging, and we made sweet, sweet love. I mean every single hole, amigo."

I cringed.

"Anyway, amigo; that night I woke up in her bed. And I'll be goddamned if that light wasn't there, just floating right at the foot of the bed. It was amazing. And the light," he held up his hand and looked at it, "the light spoke to me. And you know what it said, amigo?"

"What?"

"It said, 'Bill Wade. He is the one.'"

"BULL SHIT," I raised up and shook my head.

"No amigo. No," Peck was stern. "It did. It gave me your name. And I knew that you were the right guy to help me."

I massaged my brow and tried to separate myself from all the nonsense around me.

"I know you don't believe me," Peck said. "That's okay.

Just get a good night's rest. We're here for a reason, amigo. There are no coincidences in life. Everything happens for a reason. Tomorrow will be a wonderful day."

5

The Vampire of Moca

I tossed and turned. The next morning, when the heat in the tent became unbearable, I forced my eyes open and crawled out into the refreshing air. The campfire still burned, and I smelled coffee. After stumbling over to take a leak, I turned to spot Peck trudging toward me up a bank. Behind him, turquoise water sparkled and I caught a glimpse of a bright-orange raft bobbing up and down.

"Good morning amigo!" he called. "How are you today?"

"My face hurts," I said, wobbling over to sit on a log.

"Yeah, it hurts me, too!" he howled with laughter.

I was in no mood for jokes.

"Let me get you some coffee and breakfast," he said, plopping down next to me and fishing out some breakfast bars.

"What is that?" I said, pointing toward the raft.

"Oh that?" Peck looked over. "That's my little dinghy! I like to whip it out from time to time."

"Where did that come from?"

"I've had it all along, amigo. It's inflatable. In fact, I have two: one for you and one for me."

"And why do we need those?"

"Because right across that water, amigo," he motioned with glee, "is the most beautiful little slice of land in all of Puerto Rico; Gilligan's Island."

"Gilligan's Island? Seriously?"

"Yes sir," Peck nodded confidently. "It's a place that cleanses your body, mind and spirit. And this time of day, we'll probably have it to ourselves for a while. This is my gift to you. You'll see."

"Who do you have to kill there?"

Peck looked almost offended. "No one, amigo. This will just be a place for us to swim and float around and relax, and let mother nature work her magic on our troubled souls."

*   *   *

An hour later, I was working my way down over the precarious ground toward the raft. It looked like a child's toy, though there were a couple oars. I plopped down in it, unsure it would hold my 200 pounds. The raft sank deeply, shifting side-to-side, but held me up with unexpected firmness. The water that splashed on me was cool. It felt good.

Peck sat in his raft and giggled. "Okay amigo, follow me over to the island."

He began to oar. It took me a few minutes to coordinate the silly movements in this tiny inflatable, but soon we were both heading away from the shore. I could see a small, emerald-green island in the near distance. The water was incredibly clear and beautiful. The closer we got to the patch of uninhabited land called Gilligan's Island, the more striking and beautiful the water became. Truly, it was the most amazing, crystalline, aquamarine color I had ever seen. It looked almost radioactive.

In a short time, we were on the white, sandy beach. Far in the distance, back on the mainland, I could see mansions, but for the moment, we felt like the only people in the world. All was quiet and peaceful.

"There are channels of water that run through the mangroves on this island," Peck said. "And if you enter one of those channels, the current will take you, automatically, like a little Disney World ride, and all you have to do is lay back and relax." He crawled over toward my raft like a weird, barefoot kid. "Here."

Peck handed me a little digital audio player with ear buds. "Just put these in your ears, float away, and let all your stresses dissolve."

I didn't have the energy to question him. I popped the ear buds in. The music playing was Erik Satie's Gnossienne No. 4, same as before. Strange, haunting piano notes drowned out everything, and I drifted off down a mangrove channel. Peck was right. My spirit was being cleansed.

* * *

I'm not sure how much time passed. I didn't want to leave that raft, and when I finally did, it was like being a kid dragged out of bed to school in the morning. I squirmed up on the sand, and Peck was grilling some weenies in a little cove. Next to him was a 6-pack of sweaty, ice-cold Medallas.

"Where did you get all this shit?" I asked in wonder and bewilderment.

He just flashed his cheshire smile. "I'm an agent, dude. I have lots of tricks up my sleeve."

He pulled out a beer and I eagerly swept it from his hand. I love that little "pop," and spray of water, when you crack open an icy cerveza when you're sun-dried. The first few gulps were pure paradise. The sun was beaming down hard now, and I could hear the buzz of boats in the distance, finally bringing others over to enjoy Gilligan's Island.

"You feel cleansed now, don't you?" Peck grinned like a salesman.

I hesitated to give him any satisfaction, but I had to agree. "Yes."

"You know why that is?" he asked.

"Because it's beautiful and peaceful," I responded, my expression stressing the obvious.

"Well, that's part of it," Peck nodded with a sage-like aura, "but there's more, amigo."

There always was with him. "Uh huh, and what's that?" I asked.

"I began studying it years ago," Peck began. "Here we are, right in the middle of the Bermuda Triangle. And I wondered for years what was so special about this place. I couldn't put my finger on it until I saw some research that NASA had done. They produced a graphic of planet earth that showed the inconsistencies in the earth's gravitation field. Do you know about that?"

"Know about what?"

"The earth's gravity field is not the same everywhere, amigo. For example, a clock in your basement runs slower than a clock in your attic because the clock in your basement is closer to the earth's gravitational field, and gravity slows time. Did you know that?"

"Uhhh, kind of," I said.

"And so," he continued, "gravity is not the same everywhere. In some places it's stronger and in some places it's weaker. So NASA made this map of the earth's gravitational field and they color-coded it so that the places with high gravity were red, and the places with low gravity were blue. And in-between you have orange and yellow and shit. But anyway, of the whole planet earth, this little area we call the Bermuda Triangle is all blue. And the bluest of the blue is the island of Puerto Rico. And the bluest of the island is right around here, the west coast. It's so damn blue you can't even see it on the fucking map. Part of that is because we're close to the Puerto Rico trench, the deepest point in the Atlantic Ocean, and the second deepest point on the entire planet. It's almost 30,000 feet deep; so deep you could almost take Mount Everest and set the whole damn thing down inside it, under the ocean. So right now, you're experiencing some of the lowest gravity you have ever experienced in your entire life. Do you know what that means?"

I admitted it, I was fascinated. "No," I said. "What does that mean?"

"What happens when you're in space and there's no gravity amigo?"

I stared at him for a moment. We stared at each other. My mind was blank.

"Shit floats around!" he exclaimed. "Right?"

"Yeah."

"So guess what's happening to all the little sub-atomic particles in your brain right now . . . They're floating around. They're relaxing. They're opening up to the energies. And that's why you can come here and literally expand your mind, relax, and experience new shit, amigo." He stared at me quietly, and directly.

"Okay," I said. "I get it."

"That's why everything on this island is a big dream," Peck shook his head passionately. "Life is a dream anyway, but here it's so exaggerated—so magnified—that you get to see it's all a big dream, right before your eyes."

We sat silent for a minute. "Are those weenies ready?" I asked.

"Yeah, sure amigo," Peck reached over to make me a dog. "I don't have any mustard, though."

"That's okay," I said.

We wolfed down our dogs, then I leaned back, drowsy with relaxation. I just wanted to nap again. Then I suddenly remembered what we had done and where we were.

"Aren't they going to kill us now?" I asked. "Everyone saw what happened last night."

"Don't worry amigo," Peck reassured me. "I'm with the government dude. I can call in the cavalry any time I want. I'm just here to apply pressure. If they throw in the towel and release our little buddy, all this ends immediately. But they still haven't done that."

"And so what happens next?"

"We're gettin' close to the big kahuna, amigo," Peck kicked back and looked up at the azure sky. "In fact, there's only one more dickhead left before we get to him."

"Oh. Who's that?"

Peck sat up straight. "He's a real creepy little bastard. They call him the Vampire of Moca. Get ready to meet a fruity sex maniac who likes to drink blood. But he's the nicest guy you'll ever meet when he's fucking you in the ass."

I sighed. "Why is he called the Vampire of . . .?"

"Moca," Peck completed my thought. "Moca is little town up north. In the 70s, hundreds of cows, chickens, goats—you name it—were being mutilated and drained of blood. In retrospect, it seemed like a forerunner of the chupacabra. Most people have forgotten about that madness now, but this guy is from there, and now he runs

the area around Mayaguez. But he likes to drink blood—
human blood—so people call him the Vampire of Moca."

"And we're gonna move on to him now?"

"That's right," Peck said. "That little prick is next on my
list. And we're gonna go there, to Mayaguez, tonight."

"And what's the plan?" I asked.

"The plan?" Peck said.

"Yeah. What are we gonna do?"

"We're gonna kill the little fuck. That's the plan."

* * *

All the relaxation of Gilligan's Island seeped away as we
careened around tight, steep curves.

"Why are we going so fast?" I complained.

"Cause it's fun, amigo," Peck said. "But I do want to
stop and show you somethin'."

We pulled off onto a narrow dirt road at the top of
a hill. Slowly, we rumbled down over brown gravel, an
occasional tree dropping shade from above. Our car eased
into an opening with a breathtaking view. The bright blue
ocean spread before us. Steep cliffs soared up at the sides,
and white, frothy waves crashed against ancient boul-
ders at the water's break. It reminded me of those cheezy
scenes of lovers rolling on the sand at a sweeping, romantic beach. And in the water, just off the shore, I watched a
strange spectacle.

Four teenage Puerto Rican boys frolicked in the ocean

along with two horses. Water glistened and rolled down the horses' backs as they stomped and jumped, half-swimming and half-trotting. The whole scene was giddy. They noticed us, but seemed oblivious, clearly absorbed in some kind of physical exercise. Ultimately, though, it was just fun.

"They race those horses for big money around here," Peck said.

"Oh really?"

"Yeah. And so they take them out into the ocean and let the horses swim and stay in shape. You'd be amazed how healthy horses are when they learn to stay afloat in rough currents."

"I guess I've seen a real sea horse now," I said.

Peck slapped me on the back and guffawed, his big white teeth shining in the sun. "That's right amigo," he laughed. "You got it."

Given the things we had done, and what we were about to do, I found the entire situation odd and puzzling. Peck had been a man on a mission. But now his demeanor was different. In that moment, I felt more like we were just lost tourists that had stumbled upon some innocent window into the island culture. I must admit, it felt good. In fact, it was an escape really. For a while, I just leaned there, on the hood of the car, and pretended I was on a vacation.

When we finally left, we were back on the country roads, zooming along without a care in the world. Peck was usually quite good with navigation, but he began to grumble about the roads being wrong. I didn't pay much attention to it at first, but he kept stopping and turning around and going down other roads. "What the fuck," he would say, as if the roads had been switched on him overnight.

"Driving is such a pain the ass here," Peck said. "Have you ever driven around this island, amigo?"

"A little, but not much," I said.

"Well do you realize that all the distances on signs are written in kilometers, but all the speed limit signs are in miles per hour? How fucked up is that?"

"That's pretty weird," I said.

"All the road signs are in Spanish but this is a U.S. territory. And the gas is in liters. I think they were gonna convert all this shit to metric at some point, and then the project stopped and instead of correcting it, Puerto Rico just said FUCK IT."

"That's pretty strange," I added.

"So anywho, I'm not exactly sure where the fuck we are right now, amigo. We must have gotten off a little side road somewhere. I'm gonna need some directions." We probably drove another fifteen minutes before we finally saw someone. An old guy in overalls, wearing a big cap, was on the side of the country road. I'd never seen anyone wearing overalls here before. Peck pulled up beside him.

"Hola senor!" Peck greeted him.

"Hola!" he bellowed.

"Yo hablo muy poco Espanol. Habla Ingles?"

"Muy poco," said the man with a self-conscious smile.

"I am lost," Peck stated with a self-deprecating tone.

The old man chuckled. He spoke with a deep, monotone voice. "You never lost when you in Puerto Rico," he said. "No matter where you go, you always on the island."

Peck flashed his million-dollar smile. "Si senor! Si!"

Soon enough, thanks to the directions Peck managed to eke out of the old Puerto Rican, we were supposedly back on the right path. But Peck still seemed to think he had missed another turn somewhere, somehow.

By now, since we were in a convertible, I figured I might be getting sunburned. But I didn't care. I imagined the healing sun drying out the wound on my face. And when I closed my eyes and dropped back my head, I thought about my mother. The doctors said she had come through perfectly, without a hitch. And my sister, Miranda, asked once again when I was coming home. Christy, the girl I'd been dating when I left, was there at the hospital. She had continued hanging out with my family even though I was long gone. Her family sucked, and so I think she'd adopted my family as hers. My mom had always liked Christy, and it seemed my family had now happily adopted her, as well. I was lost in these thoughts, and then . . .

SCREEEECH! I was jarred upright. What in the name of holy hell was this?

Our car sat still in the middle of the road. Peck was silent, staring straight ahead. I shifted up and saw the reason for our sudden stop. There, in the middle of the road, was a giant monkey. It was standing almost like a man, upright. Its coat had a blondish-orange sheen; its face was stern and baboonish; its ears were white, alert tufts, and a broad white stripe ran down its front. It stood firm like an iron statue or a brick wall, offended that we were there.

We were silent. I must say, in all honesty, there was a sense that we were in the presence of something great. The monkey simply stood and looked at us. And we simply sat and looked at it. And then the monkey nodded, in the most wise, deliberate way, and ambled on across the street. Once he reached the brush at the side, he seemed to instantly vanish. Breathless, we were quiet a few moments longer. Peck looked at me.

"Did you see that?" he asked, his eyes spacey.

"Yes," I replied.

He took his hands from the wheel and plopped back as far as he could, taking a big, long breath and exhaling it. Another car zoomed by us at 100 miles per hour. The shock-wave nearly blew his hat off. I'd never seen Peck so out of it. It was obvious that seeing this monkey had made a profound impact on him. Another car zoomed by.

"Peck, we're gonna get killed here," I said.

He just sat there, frozen, a dreamy expression on his face. "Peck!"

He turned to me and smiled. "Do you know what just happened, amigo?" he spoke slowly.

"What?"

"That monkey just regarded us."

"Yeah? So?"

"He blessed us. Do you realize what that means, amigo?"

"No," I said, slightly frustrated. "What does that mean?"

"It means the spirits of the island are smiling upon us, amigo," his face spread into a grin of sheer joy. "It means we're on the right track, amigo."

Another car zoomed by. "Okay, okay," I replied. "But let's get the fuck outta the road."

"Everything is gonna go well, amigo," he stated. "Everything is gonna be okay."

With that, he pressed the accelerator and we gradually continued down the lane.

* * *

Mayaguez is a large, worn, somewhat cluttered, town on the western edge of Puerto Rico. Peck and I sat outside, on a noisy little street corner, having some drinks. "We must be insane to be out here in the open like this," I said.

"Nothing to worry about, amigo," he replied.

"How quickly could we escape from here if we needed to?"

"Well," Peck twirled the umbrella in his fruity concoction, "there's actually an airport nearby."

"Oh?"

"Yep. I used to have a friend, Niko, who worked there for many years. I flew in and out of there a few times on the smallest plane you've ever seen. You've never really experienced the miracle of flight till you sit in a little chair in the clouds and glide over this fantastic little island."

"I've always been a little freaked out by flying," I said. "I try not to think about all the empty space below my seat."

"I once asked Niko how many planes had crashed at that little airport. He told me, in over thirty years, there had been only one. A rather gruff pilot, alone in his own little plane, was coming in to land. But they'd been watching the weather at the airport and saw some extremely dangerous patterns. There were some notorious currents at work, and so they told him not to land. 'Oh, I can do it,' said the pilot. They told him again, 'don't land.' Be he insisted. They kept begging him and begging him, and then finally, the pilot said, 'I'm comin' in!' Then he crashed like a motherfucker and died, right on the runway, in a ball of fire."

I sat there for a moment thinking about the scene, and then I burst into laughter. Peck started to laugh, too, and soon, we were both crying with twisted humor. It was obvious that we were frazzled and sleep-deprived.

"I'm comin' in!" I exclaimed, howling with more laughter.

"I wonder what that guy was like in bed?" Peck added. "I'm comin' in!"

We laughed and laughed, as if it were the funniest thing in the world.

After we finally settled a bit, Peck asked "Are you into baseball?"

"Mmmm, not really," I said.

"Have you ever heard of Roberto Clemente?"

"Yeah, yeah, I've heard of him," I said.

"Well he was a Puerto Rican," Peck ran his finger around the rim of his glass. "He was born in Carolina, near San Juan. And he was one helluva baseball player. Everyone loved him, and he was very charitable, always helping out people in need. I think it was . . .1972 when he took a vacation to Nicaragua and had a wonderful time. And right after that, an earthquake hit Nicaragua, and the people there were in dire trouble. So Clemente loaded an airplane with disaster relief goodies and sent it down there. But it didn't make it because some corrupt government assholes got it instead. So he loaded up another. Same thing happened to it. And a third one! And so, finally, Clemente loaded up a fourth plane and decided that he, himself, would personally go on the plane to make sure it arrived where it belonged to help the people. He felt they wouldn't mess with it because of his celebrity. And so the plane took off from San Juan, and it immediately crashed into the ocean, killing everyone. And that is how the great baseball player, Roberto Clemente died, when he was just 38 years old. His body was never found."

"Why did it crash?" I asked.

"I don't know," Peck stated. "But do you get the moral of that story amigo?"

"What?" I asked.

"Sometimes you're just fucked, dude," Peck spoke with

barroom brilliance. "He was fucked, they were fucked. Everybody was fucked. Sometimes, if it's meant to be, try all you may, but you're all still fucked. But the good news is that it also works the other way around. Sometimes, when all the odds seem to be against you, you're destined to prevail. And that's why I don't worry, amigo, and neither should you."

"You're not even worried a little bit about El Brujo?" I squinted skeptically.

Peck grinned sheepishly, as if he were impressed by my perceptiveness. "I must admit, he is the only guy who really scares the shit outta me," Peck grimaced. "He's Hitler and Darth Vader combined. If there actually is a devil, it's this magical bastard. He's the kinda guy who fucks up your whole family for fun. He doesn't kill you. He keeps you alive in a box for years and does shit that makes your skin crawl. He wants your body and soul. That's why he runs every dark, depraved evil enterprise on this side of the globe."

We were silent for a bit more; reflective. "And yet you don't want me to worry?" I snapped.

Peck blew me off. "One thing at a time, amigo. Now we must focus on The Vampire. And if we're lucky, El Brujo will give in and release our little friend once he realizes he's next on my list."

* * *

Most towns in Puerto Rico have a little village square they call a Plaza. It's pretty much what you imagine; just a rectangular space, with a church at one end, that serves as the focus of official activity. It's the hub of each weekend, often focused on musical performances, where old people relax and young people dream about their future lives. These plazas look the same as they did a hundred years ago, a magnificent statue in the middle. In Mayaguez, they call their center Plaza Colon. In the heart is a statue of Columbus, his noble face eyeing the unseen potential on the horizon.

Peck and I strolled around the plaza as the afternoon grew late and the sun settled in the distance. A mystical light softly reflected off everything as we passed the statues. I felt uneasy.

"What makes you think we're not being targeted right now?" I asked Peck.

"Think about it, amgio," he said. "El Brujo keeps his men very separated, so there's a good chance the right hand doesn't know what the left hand is doing. But more importantly: drug dealers are always fighting violence, so they wouldn't necessarily connect the dots to know that the same dudes are going around and fucking them all up. These guys are only keeping track of their own territories, so they're not seeing the big picture. It's like a big magic trick."

I stared up at the clear sky. "Looks like it will be a nice sunset tonight," I said.

"I'm glad you said that amigo," Peck's face brightened. "We should drive over to the water and watch it. Maybe we'll see the green flash."

"What's that?" I asked.

"Here, get in the car and I'll tell you when we get there," he said.

* * *

Soon enough we were in a nice little windy park, right beside the Mayaguez Bay. It seemed like we had the whole place to ourselves as the sun was clearly descending over the sea. Every ripple of the water shined like a gentle, liquid-metal wave.

"Did you know there are a shitload of earthquakes on this island every week amigo?" Peck asked.

"No," I said.

"Yeah, the last big one was in 1918. And it's now known as the," his voice became dramatic, "Great Tsunami of 1918. Did you know that, amigo?"

"No," I replied, staring out to sea. "I've never heard of that."

"Oh yeah," Peck shook his head knowingly. "It was a 7.5 right off the coast. In some places, the wave that blasted in was almost twenty feet tall. 116 people died that day. I'd say we got off lucky. And you know how all the scientists are always saying that someday, any day, the big one is gonna hit California? Well they say the same thing is gonna happen here in Puerto Rico. It could happen to us any second; even right now as we stand here on this shore. And we'd most likely be fucked."

"Oh," I said. "Well that's a nice thought."

"Okay, watch the sun as it goes down," Peck was stiff and alert again, leaning somewhat against a lamp post. "Don't blink or you'll miss it."

"What is the green flash?" I asked.

"It's just a green flash of light right as the sun is going down," he said. "It doesn't always happen, but I've seen it many times from right here. And never have we needed it more than tonight, amigo."

"Why is that?"

"Because if it happens, right in front of you, it gives you the strength of the sun, just like Superman. And we are up against vampires tonight, amigo."

"Vampires aren't fucking real. These are just wackos who drink blood, right?" I shrugged.

"Don't look away from the sun!" Peck commanded.

"Okay, okay!" I shot my head back to the burning yellow ball. It hurt my eyes.

"I'm not sure," Peck said. "I know the Vampire of Moca drinks blood. He's very rich, and he's probably gay."

"That figures," I said.

"What figures?" asked Peck.

"Most rich men are gay," I replied.

Peck was quiet for a moment. "What's makes you say that, amigo?" He sounded puzzled.

"Have you ever met trophy wives? They're so annoying that no straight man could put up with them. They must just be for show."

"Hmm," Peck nodded. "You've just opened my mind a little amigo. OH SHIT!" he exclaimed. "Did you see it?"

Sure enough, just before the last golden sliver of sun slipped below the watery horizon, a neon-green light, like an old camera flashbulb, popped into the colors of the sky. Sure enough, if I had blinked, I would have missed it. I finally closed my eyes, and realized the sun was burned into the back of my eyelids.

"I think my eyes are fucked up," I said. "You're not supposed to look at the sun."

"You're fine, dude," Peck assured me. "Just remember that image tonight when you need to call upon pure solar strength to defeat darkness."

Yeah. Whatever.

* * *

It was nice and dark when we returned to Plaza Colon. The mood was very different now. A variety of Egyptian figures stood stoically as bearers of lamps. And noble lights featured Columbus, triumphantly poised atop his pedestal in the center, fierce, old-world lions at his feet, and jets of illuminated water spurting up below.

"You know somethin'?" Peck said, leaning back to peer up at the statue. "When Columbus came here, he wrote that the Taino Indians were the most gentle people in the world, always laughing and generous and kind. But only a year later, if a Taino 14 years old or older wasn't providing enough gold and cotton to the Spaniards, every time they visited, those bastards would cut off their hands and leave them to bleed to death. And now look, here is Columbus, celebrated all over the island."

Despite what Peck had said, everything in the Plaza was quite pleasant. Oddly enough, someone had placed an upright piano out near a snack stand, and random folks could have a seat to tinkle out a tune. Some of them were quite talented, even a couple of kids. A small group of men were also in the process of setting up a large screen and a number of folding chairs. We grabbed a seat and relaxed for an hour. A baseball game was being projected on the screen, and delighted residents sipped coffee and nibbled candy as they watched the show.

"Okay," Peck finally looked at his watch, "let's take a little walk."

We worked our way around a couple streets, but not too far from the plaza really. Up ahead, I could see eerie purplish-blue lights casting a ghastly glow on the dark street. The light came from the partly-obscured windows of a secluded bar. It appeared to be at least two stories tall. Peck opened the door. "After you," he bowed.

I walked into a strange, but cool, bar. A stout Puerto Rican man sat on a stool.

"Hola," he said.

"Hi," I said. Peck stepped inside.

"Do you have a membership?" he asked.

Peck tipped down his glasses and looked him dead in the eye. "Margarita sent me."

"Oh, okay," said the man, and waved us on through.

It was quite open inside. I could look up and see people conversing on the balconies of the second floor. The lower floor had a couple pool tables. Some fellas, who looked a bit rough, were deeply involved in the billiard tables. And yet all around the floor were tall tavern tables, with people scarfing down thick, juicy cheeseburgers. We sauntered over to the bar and plopped down under a black light advertising DonQ Coco rum. There were two bartenders. One was an attractive girl with long, black hair pulled into a ponytail. The other was a slim, but kind of buff, dude. They both wore tight black t-shirts. I was hoping the chick would approach us first, but it was the guy.

"Buenas," he said with a smile. Then, with a bit of an accent, "welcome. How can I help you?"

"Hello sir," Peck grinned. "I would like a DonQ Coco rum with pineapple juice."

"No problem. And you?" he looked to me.

"Uh . . . I'll just have a Medalla," I said.

The bartender happily turned and walked to make our drinks. I looked over at Peck. He took a big breath, and looked extremely relaxed, turning on his stool to soak in the action of the room. I did the same. As I slowly scanned around, I sensed something weird. There were quite a few tough-looking guys in the room, tucked away into various shadows and absorbed in various discussions. Some paid attention to us and others did not. They didn't really look out of place, and yet there was indeed something about them that was odd. I couldn't put my finger on it.

"Nice place, huh?" Peck said.

"Yeah," I replied. "But there's something unusual about it. I'm not sure what it is."

"Well look," Peck said matter-of-factly, "all these motherfuckers have babies."

Huh? Instantly, my perspective switched. He was right. How the fuck had I missed it. Here we were in a bar, at night, with men drinking all over the place, yet many of them had small kids, often toddlers. "Is there a birthday party going on?" I asked.

"I dunno," Peck said. "I've noticed a lot of Puerto Ricans will just dress up and go out to bars and take their little kids with them. I've seen 'em strolling babies at 2 in the morning. But there could be a party here." Peck looked up at the balcony directly above us. There were people buzzing around with drinks in their hands, completely oblivious to us below.

The bartender brought back our drinks. "How do I get upstairs?" Peck asked.

"Oh, there's a staircase," said the bartender, "but tonight there's a private party up there."

"Ah, okay," Peck said. "How much do we owe you?"

"Umm, it'll be eight dollars," he said.

Peck took out his wallet and pulled out a stack of hundred dollar bills. He flipped through, taking his time. "I think I have a ten in here somewhere," he seemed frustrated. I saw the eyes of the bartender sparkle a bit.

"Ahh, here we go," Peck slapped down a ten.

"Thank you," said the bartender, then he left us to enjoy our drinks.

"We need to get up there," Peck said, motioning to the balcony and floor above us.

"Okay," I said. "That's where the real party is, huh?"

"Probably," Peck replied. "Go find out," he said.

"What?"

"Just go walk up the steps and see how far you can get. When someone finally asks who you are, just say you're looking for the bano. That's Spanish for bathroom."

"Yeah, I know," I said.

I walked off toward the banos, passed them, and took a left up the stairs. When I reached the top, I saw a lot of slim guys, covered in jewelry, drinking in the shadows. A guy tending the bar at the top of the steps looked at me, along with a couple patrons.

"Hello. Can I help you?"

"Yeah, I'm looking for the banos."

"Oh, okay. They're right back down the stairs and to your left."

"Ah," I played dumb. "I must have just walked right by

them. Gracia." I turned and shuffled back down the steps. I popped into the bathroom, took a leak, then emerged and took my seat back next to Peck again.

"Well?" asked Peck.

"It's just a bunch of sleazy, shady-looking guys, covered in jewelry. They're just drinking and hanging out. It didn't look like a birthday party though."

"Did you notice if they were wearing a lot of crosses?"

"Crosses?"

"Yeah, crucifixes and stuff," Peck said.

I had to pause and think for a moment, conjuring up the image I had seen. "Yeah, actually. I do think I remember seeing some big-ass blingy crosses."

"Good," said Peck.

"But aren't vampires supposed to not like crosses?" I said.

"They're not real vampires dipshit," Peck said.

"Yeah, but . . . but earlier I said . . ."

Peck cut me off. "Just listen, amigo. We need to get up there." He threw his head back to look right over top of us, and I did the same. Directly above our heads, two men were leaned up against the balcony, drinks in hand, chatting away with each other.

"Have you ever done cloud-busting, amigo?" Peck asked.

"No. What is that?"

"It's when you look at a cloud and you think to it, over and over, that you want it to break into pieces. And then, in a few minutes, right before your eyes, it happens. The cloud breaks apart. You've never done that?"

"No, I haven't."

"Okay, well we're gonna do something similar here, amigo." I could tell Peck was getting fired up. "We're gonna just stare up at those guys and we're gonna think to them, really hard, you want us to be up there with you. Okay?"

"You mean like some Jedi mind shit?" I said.

"Yeah," Peck said. "A mind fuck."

"Okay," I played along.

We sat back and stared up at those guys. It felt weird, and I wondered how long we could do this until someone pointed out that we were acting awkward. I began to feel a little irritated. Why the fuck were we doing this? Obviously, nothing was going to happen. It wasn't like those guys would see us staring up and then go, "Oh. Hey, you! You guys come up here and join us. Please!" It was pointless. And yet, right as that thought entered my mind, something remarkable happened.

The guy standing above us to the right looked a lot like Count Chocula. He had a long, thin nose and swept-back hair. Gold bracelets dangled from his left wrist, and his left hand held a plastic cup of liquor. He was carried away in conversation, and amazingly, right there before my eyes, his cup just slipped smoothly right out of his hand. It was almost like slow motion as it fell down and exploded on the bar inches before us, a cold spray of rum and club soda splashing me and Peck like the shock of a shattered water balloon. I looked at Peck to see beads of liquid dripping off the lenses of his sunglasses and the brim of his hat. And on his face, a wiley smile unfolded.

We looked up to see an expression of horror and embarrassment on Count Chocula's visage. He immediately rushed away from the railing, and the bartender scrambled to fling napkins on us and wipe the bar in broad, desperate strokes. As we wiped down, Count Chocula was there in a flash. His hands were on Peck's shoulders, and he rambled with apologies.

"Oh my God," Chocula was saying. "Lo Siento! So very, very sorry! Oh no! This has never happened before!" He was helping to wipe us both down in whatever way he could.

Peck looked displeased, but he was nice. "It's no problem, amigo. I know it was an accident," he said. "I just hope my wallet isn't wet." Peck opened his wallet and started pulling out the stacks of hundred dollar bills, wiping them down with napkins. Chocula definitely took notice.

"I will buy you a drink, my friend!" Chocula exclaimed. "Oh," he closed his eyes. "I can't believe this. I'm so sorry, so very, very sorry. What can I get you, my friend?"

"What are you guys drinkin' up there?" Peck asked.

"Oh, we have a nice bar!" Chocula exclaimed. "Whatever you want! Whatever you want. Please, come on up and be my guest. Let me buy you a new drink." Chocula nodded to our bartender, and the bartender returned the gesture. With that, we were ushered upstairs, exactly in the middle of this private party, and exactly where Peck envisioned we would be.

We sat at a dim table. There must have been fifty men up there. All looked Puerto Rican, with black hair, and jewelry glistening everywhere. Indeed, almost every man had at least one large cross hanging from his neck. Some were silver, some were gold, and some bedazzled with jewels.

"My name is Raoul," Chocula said in the most humble way.

"I'm Peck," Peck said.

"And I'm Bill," I said.

"What can I get you two gentlemen to drink?"

"Just a DonQ Coco and pineapple for me," Peck replied.

"And I'll have the same," I said. Peck looked at me strangely for a moment, as if I'd stumbled onto his territory.

"No problem, amigos," Raoul said. He called to the bartender to bring our drinks. "And are you on vacation?" he asked Peck.

"Yeah, we are," Peck said. "I just got divorced, so I came to San Juan on vacation with my buddy. We rented a car, and I love this place. I won $10,000 at the casino today, so I am ready to party hearty!"

"Oh my goodness," Raoul said. "You won $10,000?" I realized just how long and willowy his limbs and fingers were, and how smoothly he moved. He actually looked like he could be related to Don Quixote.

"Yes, I hit the goddman progressive!" Peck laughed roughly, just as the drinks arrived.

"Ah, cheers!" said Raoul.

"Salud!" cried Peck as we bumped cups then downed a swig.

A variety of other dark figures walked over and Raoul introduced us to each one. Most were not fluent in English, and we mingled with sheer small talk for a while.

"So, how do you want to celebrate your winning tonight?" Raoul finally asked.

"The three double-ues," Peck said. "Wine, women and weed!"

"Ahh!" Raoul slapped his knee and laughed with sincere glee. "Of course! What better way?"

"That's my style," Peck sounded naïve.

"Well," Raoul sat up straight, "I know where you can find all three!"

"Really?" Peck perked up, too.

"Yes indeed."

"Where?"

"Ummm," Raoul appeared to be searching for the right words. "You have a car?"

"Yes."

"You would need to follow me. It's in another town nearby."

"And that's where the real party is?" Peck sounded a slight bit skeptical.

"Ohhh yes!" Raoul said. "The best party in Puerto Rico. I promise you."

"Excellent," Peck sipped his beverage.

"But," Raoul raised a finger, "I need to know how much you are willing to spend. I'm not allowed to take you there otherwise."

"I understand," Peck pooched out his bottom lip and opened his wallet. He thumbed five hundred dollar bills onto the table. "Hell I hit the jackpot today, and I'm in a generous mood. Here's five hundred dollars for you, amigo."

"Really?" Raoul seemed like he couldn't believe it.

"Really," Peck stated.

"Okay then," Raoul swept up the money. "Let's go amigo. You can follow me. We're going to a very old town called San German." It was pronounced like San Her-mon.

* * *

The drive to San German was spooky. We maneuvered on dark back roads, and the beams of our headlights continually morphed, like white phantoms, off the trunk of every tree, and edge of every leaf, we passed. Raoul zoomed ahead of us in a sporty little black number, whipping around each curve. Eventually, we ascended a steep, bumpy hill, and entered a scenic little plaza. Parking was tricky, since the edge of the authentic cobblestone plaza was a trough, a few inches deep, to keep heavy rainwater at bay. If one accidentally pulled into it, it could bend a car axle. We were the only people on the streets. It looked like a ghost town, despite the dramatic lighting.

We hopped out and I spun 360 degrees. This town looked like an illustration in a storybook. Right behind us, perched atop a walkway of brick steps, a lit, stark-white chapel glowed in the gloom of night above us. It was a simple, but elegant, shape: an arched door set beneath an angled roof with a crumble of ruins at its side.

"That is Porta Coeli, the portal to heaven," Raoul called as he exited his car and slammed the door. "It was built in 1609. Isn't it magnificent?"

"Yeah," I called back. "It's incredible."

"I am glad you like it!" he said.

Peck and I were silent for a bit, just taking in the beauty of this new town together.

"San German used to be the western capital of Puerto Rico. Now it's just a nice little town," Raoul walked toward us. "But there is the university nearby, and so there are a lot of young people who like to party here," he said.

"Where are they all?" Peck asked.

Raoul laughed sardonically. "That is what I am here to show you, amigo! Here, follow me to the top of the steps."

Raoul raced effortlessly up the ancient brick stairs to Porta Coeli. We followed him. At the top, we turned to soak in a magnificent perspective. Even though it was dark, the lighted layout of the plaza before us was striking, and a house, just on the corner below, looked like the most classic "haunted house" you can imagine, with a sprawling deck and pointed turrets.

"Is nice, huh?" Raoul giggled.

"Yes!" Peck said. "Very nice."

"So look off far into the distance and you can barely see bits of another church way back there in another plaza, yes?"

Indeed, we could see a few structures protruding that were obviously of a church.

"Well," Raoul continued, "way back beyond that church, there is another church. And according to legend, there was a group of nuns who could never show their faces because they were not yet holy enough. If you glimpsed them in public, you would only see a cloister of ladies covered in head to foot with black cloth. And so they would travel all the way from that church, where they stayed, to Porta Coeli, through tunnels that are underneath this town. And now, their phantasmas—their ghosts—haunt the tunnels of this city to this very day."

"Is that true, amigo?" Peck asked.

Raoul laughed. "I honestly do not know for sure, my friend. But it is in these tunnels where you will find the party. And most of the people who live here—who have lived here their entire lives—actually have no idea that this party exists in these tunnels at night. SO you should think about how special it is for me to bring you to this."

"I understand amigo," Peck said, "and it kicks ass."

"Okay then—follow me," Raoul motioned, and we walked down the steps and over toward the big, creepy-ass, haunted-looking house.

Just below the house, on the backside, was a black,

wrought-iron gate. It squeaked as we slipped through and meandered through the high grass of an unkempt yard. It looked like a little set of steps went down into a cellar. This type of configuration was unusual for Puerto Rico. It looked more like the kind of thing my folks did in Tennessee. We all lowered our heads to keep from banging them on the heavy stone slabs above, and I realized we were truly entering a hidden portal to a new lair.

Raoul took out his cell phone and used it as a flashlight. After taking a few careful steps down, I could hear the thumping of music below us. With a few more steps, I could hear the laughter of a joyous party crowd. Sure enough, there was obviously something big happening deep below the streets.

Eventually we reached a black obstacle. I assumed it was a door. Though I couldn't tell exactly what was happening, it appeared Raoul had reached up into a corner and banged a metal knocker a few times. Aside from his cell light, I could see nothing. We waited for a few moments, then he did it again. Knock. Knock, knock, knock. Knock knock.

Suddenly the metal obstacle was indeed a door that cracked open with a jar. "Si?" we heard from other side.

Raoul leaned down. "Margarita," he said, and then the door opened wider. Holy fuck. That really was the password all over this island.

The door opened and we were in party central. The song Happy Up Here by Royksopp was blasting as we entered the kaleidoscope of colors and darkness. I was in a sea of young people, lost in a haze of smoke and hedonism. Young men and women were clustered everywhere, bumping, grinding and staggering, drinking straight from bottles of rum and whiskey. All around were people snorting and shooting drugs into their arms. It was the most sad and pitiful display I'd ever seen of smiling, laughing people clouding their senses with sin.

"Welcome amigos!" Raoul screamed, giddy, his eyes already rolling with joy, obviously thinking of the things this night would hold. "Have a strong drink!"

Peck began waving his hips, dancing around into the crowd like he belonged there. Young women, intrigued but hapless, were already moving in around him. I held back a bit.

"Pitorro for mi amigios!" Raoul shouted to the bartender just inside the doorway.

In short order, Raoul had two glasses in his hands filled with clear liquid. "Here! Here! Is like local moonshine!" he forced one into my hand, then tracked down Peck and handed him one, as well. Peck was being happily swallowed up by the dance crowd. I looked to him, and he raised his glass of pitorro approvingly, downing it in a flash. I realized that we were indeed here to party, so I shot mine as well. It was strong as hell with a coconut edge.

What happened next was cloudy, and I remember much of it in flashes. There were two hot chicks, with long blonde hair and big boobs, rubbing on me and Peck. I remember that one of them said to Peck she was a spiritual massage therapist. She asked if he had a problem with his yin/yang energy.

"Yeah, I have a yin/yang problem!" he said. "I need somebody to suck on my yang!"

One of the chicks said her name was Melanie, and started screaming in my ear about how her dad had a boat and had sailed down to Puerto Rico from Boston. I can't recall most of what she was saying, but she was definitely flirting. I hadn't experienced that in a long time since most Puerto Rican chicks don't seem to care for gringos.

I kept my eye on Peck, though it was hard. He was actually getting in the middle of this madness and cutting a rug. I looked up and examined the wicked arched stones above us. This area could have been a sewer in the past. It looked cool as hell. I lost Peck for a while, ordered another drink and decided to enjoy myself.

"Here!" Melanie said. She had a joint in her hand. I took a deep drag, held it, and blew out the smoke. HOLY SHIT was I fucked up after that. Peck walked back around, grinding his hips joyfully.

Melanie looked at Peck. "I like your hat," she said.

"Grassy-ass!" exclaimed Peck.

"Do you always wear it?"

"Why yes, I do."

"Can I wear it?"

"Sorry little lady. I might need it. When it rains it

keeps off the water, when it's hot it keeps off the sun, and whenever I run outta money, I just do this." Peck suavely flipped it off his head, and in one, smooth motion, was holding it out, upside down, like a beggar. She giggled. Peck flipped it back on his head and danced his way again into, and through, the bumping group of giddy youth.

I kept hanging there with Melanie, marveling at her assets. She kept talking as if she were a fascinating wealth of knowledge. However, her voice was just the right pitch to stay lost in the background noise. I just kept on saying, "yes," and "no" and "that's cool," even though I couldn't understand what the fuck she was saying. It seemed to work rather well though. Each time I gave a response, she reacted as if I'd responded the right way. That's as close to a psychic skill as I'd ever mastered in life.

Eventually Peck popped up again. "This is Vlad," he said. I looked over to see a small man in black clothes with extremely well-manicured eyebrows. His hair was coal-black, and gold and diamond jewels hung from all over his body. His face looked soft and smooth—almost baby-like—and his earrings sparkled like stars. He extended a limp hand and smiled sheepishly.

"Hi," I shouted over the music. "Bill!"

I couldn't actually hear his voice, but his lips mouthed "Nice to meet you." He batted his eyes.

"Come on!" Peck yelled.

"Huh?" I replied, half-hearing him.

"Come with me!" Peck shouted.

"I'll be right back," I said to Melanie. At that point, I realized Vlad had Peck by the hand and was leading him off. I was following. Was this the Vampire of Moca?

We shoved our way through the crowd and twisted through ancient hallways.

"I've seen the Camuy Caverns," Peck called back, "but this place is amazing!"

As we walked farther, the music in the background dwindled. The predominant sound was water running down the walls in artificial fountains, as candles and torches lit the way. We finally stood outside a thick curtain, guarded by a tall man with dreamy eyes.

"Okay," Vlad said. "This is the room where we really have the fun. Okay?" His voice was high-pitched, smooth and hypnotic.

"Si amigo!" Peck bellowed.

"But before you can go in here," Vlad said, "I need you to pull your cock out."

"What?" Peck asked, then shot his head toward me.

"I need to know you're not policia," Vlad said.

"All right—here!" Peck unzipped his shorts and pulled out his dick. I took a good look. I gotta be honest, it was pretty long.

Vlad looked down, smiled, and then looked up at me.

"Okay. He's good. Now you," he said.

I looked at Peck. "Pull your cock out, son," he said.

"Fine," I said. My dick is actually quite large; probably 8 inches (in my opinion). I unzipped my pants and aggressively pulled it out. It was a shriveled little 2-inch worm. Vlad and Peck literally laughed. I shoved it back inside.

"Okay, you're fine," Vlad said. "I know you're not policia!" Vlad and Peck laughed like a motherfucker. I smiled.

"Okay," said Vlad, "come on in."

Vlad slipped through the curtains. I could see another candle-lit room inside. Peck passed through next. As I passed through, I was surprised by how heavy the thick, velvet curtains were.

Once we were inside, I was standing within a huge, extensive, underground area. There was no one else there. A handful of baby carriages were strewn around, and a thin red hose was attached to each still, silent, sleeping baby, connected to a shiny, silver machine.

"Why the hell do you have all the baby dolls?" Peck asked.

Vlad chuckled. "They are not baby dolls, silly. These are the babies."

"What babies?" Peck asked.

"These are the babies I told you about."

Peck seemed thoroughly confused for a moment. "I don't know what you're talking about, amigo," he said. "Are these real babies?"

"Yes," said Vlad. "I told you that. You don't remember?" There was a green, cushioned bed at the front of the cave, and he plopped down on it. "They're okay. We're just taking blood from them. They're all okay."

I was getting the fuck outta this room. I started to say something, but then I just turned and walked out very quickly. It was an instinct, and something that struck a chord I had never felt in life. I walked as quickly and firmly as I could right back into the cluster of partying students. A hand grabbed me from the crowd. It was Melanie.

"Hey!" she shouted. "Dance with me!" My instinct was to just leave, but I knew I couldn't leave Peck behind. I waded into the crowd of fucked up people and danced with her. She was wearing a short skirt and she grinded her leg and ass all around my body. Dubstep music, its deep, resounding tones pumped and rolled all around me. I allowed myself to be swallowed back up into her world. I remember taking some more drags of a joint, and my mind flowing into another dreamlike state. The music filled my ears and consciousness. I was swept away. I can't remember how long I was in the middle of this squirming orgy of people when I was finally grabbed on the shoulder. I turned to see Peck covered in dark blood.

His eyes looked wild with violence. "Let's go," he said. I walked off with him.

"Don't go!" Melanie called. "Please!"

But my logical mind was in touch with why we had been there, and the gist of our mission. I knew Peck had most likely killed him. I swiftly followed Peck through the crowd, bouncing between the partiers, back to the same door we had entered. The door was tended by a weird-looking little man with askew eyes. When he saw us approaching, he stepped to the side and opened it without hesitation. We passed through and stomped up the steps. I was now becoming used to this feeling of running away from a crime scene.

Once we cleared the top of the steps, I took a deep breath of the cool, refreshing night air.

"Come on," Peck said, rushing off toward the car. At that point, I knew he had indeed killed his target.

We jumped into the car. He backed up in a hurry, the wheels almost falling into the rain gulley, then we tore away into the night.

"So Vlad was the Vampire?" I called above the evening wind.

"Yeah. That was the guy," he said. "I killed the FUCK outta him."

Peck drove the car hard as hell through the back roads. I was still messed up from the weed and booze, so I really didn't know exactly what was going on. As usual, Peck knew the campsites around the island, and he found a place for us to pull over and supposedly regroup our thoughts.

Peck got out of the car and walked to the water quickly as hell. I'd never seen him move that fast. It seemed that whatever he needed to wash off was particularly disturbing to him. He came back a few minutes later, having stripped off his clothes, and proceeded to go back washing again and again.

He finally walked back over, exhausted. "So Vlad was the Vampire of Moca. Right?" I asked.

"Yes," he said. "That was the son-of-a-bitch."

"And how did you kill him?" I asked.

"Well," Peck sat down on a fallen log, "he was draining the blood from babies. You saw that."

"Yes, I did," I said.

"And he said he wanted to drink my blood, and then wanted me to drink his blood."

"Okay."

"So we went over and sat down on his little green couch and he took out a syringe. He stuck the syringe in his arm and drew out blood and asked me to drink it. I've drank lots of blood from killed animals on hunting trips, but I've never drank human blood, and I was afraid his was diseased. So I said 'sure' and I took the syringe like I was gonna drink it, then I stabbed him in the fucking eyeballs with it. It was kind of like the Garadiablo with the goddamn pincho sticks in his eyes. The music was playing so loud in the background, no one could hear him scream. So I stabbed him a few times in the eyes then I put my hand over his mouth and I did something amazing. I reached down and literally shoved my hand into his throat. And he was choking and convulsing, then I just took my other hand and reached right down and pulled his fucking nuts off!" Peck laughed hysterically. "I literally pulled his nuts off!"

I felt queasy.

"Then I pulled my hand out," Peck resumed, "and his teeth cut me. Look at this!" He held up his left hand.

There were two deep cuts running down his arm, below his knuckles. "His fuckin' teeth had been sharpened, or filed, or whatever into points. That's how crazy that asshole was." There was still blood seeping from the wounds.

"So," Peck continued, "he was coughing and blood was running out of his eyes and you know what he did? You know what that little fucker started doing?"

"What?" I asked, cringing from the answer.

"He started saying the Lord's Prayer. Can you believe it? This asshole was drinking baby blood in his den and yet when his eyes were stabbed out and his balls were ripped off, he started choking and reciting the Lord's Prayer. 'Our father, who art in heaven, hallowed be thy name'. I thought to myself, you little fuckin' asshole. I hope the Lord doesn't redeem your rotten ass. And then I just started punching him and I looked over and noticed a little knife he had near the couch, made of carved bone. I've always wanted to actually spill somebody's guts. In fact, I read somewhere that happened in the Bible one time. So anyway, I took the knife and spilled his guts. I must have hit an artery somehow, because blood sprayed up all over me. His intestines came falling out. Then I just started ripping out his guts. He kept on squawling and hollering, so then I just cut his fuckin' throat and killed him. That was the end of that piece of shit."

"I think I'm gonna throw up," I whispered, the wave of sickness already rising up from my stomach to my vocal chords.

"Don't throw up," Peck snapped. "Be a man. He lived by the sword and he died by it. That's what happens to these sorry assholes when it's time to pay the piper. Here," he reached out and shoved something in my hand. "Take this."

I opened my hand to see a little, bloody blob. "What is it?" I trembled.

"It's his ball," Peck replied. "One of them."

I immediately dropped it on the ground, and heaved in deeply, trying hard to repress the nausea crawling through my abdomen.

"Don't drop it!" Peck immediately fell to his knees and scrambled around in the dirt to find it.

"Why . . ." I took a deep breath. "Why did you keep that?"

Peck rose with the testicle in his hand. "Damnit! It's dirty now!" he exclaimed, brushing the dry soil away from the gooey blood coating. "This is very valuable to us."

I took a step back. "And how is that valuable to us?"

"Because these drug dealers are superstitious as hell. That's why they wear crosses, and say prayers, and sacrifice animals, and do their little rituals. They're so greedy and obsessed they'll do anything they can, no matter how crazy, if they think it'll give them an edge and keep them alive or out of prison."

"Okay," I said. "So how does that help us exactly?"

"Because this is very powerful to El Brujo. This will

defeat his magic. And we're gonna need all the help we can get if we have to fight that bastard."

"How is a man's fucking ball gonna do anything? Listen to yourself! You sound crazy!" I exploded.

Peck suddenly stood up very straight, and he spoke with a lowered voice. "I am not crazy," he spoke firmly. "I am just aware of things that you are not aware of. You don't understand the black magic these men use. I do. And so I fight fire with fire amigo. That is how we will succeed and hopefully get our little friend back."

There was a threatening, and threatened, tone in his voice, so I backed off a bit. "Why am I even here anymore?" I asked. "You don't need me."

"Of course I do," Peck said. "You have good energy, and you're a good man to get my back if shit hits the fan. You're from Tennessee."

"But I'm a criminal!" I exclaimed.

"YES," Peck stressed. "And I'm giving you another chance in life. Only a criminal could have a stomach to help me beat these bastards. You can't do it if you play by the book. That's why I'm with a secret agency. And when we're done with this island, you'll have a new start. I believe it. Do you believe it?"

I plopped down in the dirt.

"Do you believe it?" Peck asked again, a gentler tone in his voice.

I just stared up at him. "I don't know," I confessed. "I don't know what is gonna happen."

Peck sighed. "Okay then. Let's just sit down, chill the fuck out, drink some beer, and get some sleep. You wanna help me put this tent up?"

"Yeah, sure," I said unenthusiastically.

Peck held up the testicle. "Balls are good luck," he reassured me.

* * *

Peck snored a lot that night. For me, the nightmares had returned. The mixture of drugs, liquor and demons chewed on me in the darkness of our tent. It was a claustrophobic hell. I sweated, rubbed my coarse hair, and flipped back and forth, from side-to-side. Each organ inside my body was restless. Bouts of paranoia and dread flooded over me again and again. Eventually, I was worn down by sheer exhaustion. When I finally slept, it was a deep slumber. I could feel myself sinking into the ground, and then falling faster and faster into a rush of blackness. I felt like I was dying. I wanted to go back and do everything differently— live my life in a new way. But I was hopeless now. I silently prayed to Jesus with all my heart, asking over and over again, incessantly, for a deliverance. But I knew, so painfully I knew, that it would not be granted. I was paying for my sins now. Maybe this truly was hell.

* * *

As usual, I awoke when the tent was so hot and stuffy I couldn't stand it. As the unforgiving sun rose, the green canvas glowed around me like a dull emerald. I finally squirmed upright. There were thick covers around me. I had never needed them for warmth, just to cushion my aching bones, especially my knees knocking against each other. And yet, it seemed I had pulled the blankets over me, burying myself inside like a quivering little marmot. The steam of my sweat filled the small space.

My head ached, and my vision swirled as I crawled forward pitifully to unzip the entrance, crouch and rise up through the flaps. I staggered up and squinted, the brightness like painful darts shooting into my skull. Instantly, a hard, unflinching object, about the size of a dime, firmly tapped the back of my head.

"Don't move or I will kill you," a man's Puerto Rican voice said calmly from behind. I froze. There was obviously a gun to the back of my head. Someone jerked my hands behind my back and began tying them up, winding the thin rope over and over again. My heart was pounding and I could hardly breathe. A hard force then knocked my body forward onto the ground. My face smashed against the dirt, and the cell phone in my pocket made a crunching sound. They were now tying up my feet. My eyes were squished by my cheeks, but my head was turned painfully to the left. There, on the ground next to me, was Peck, bound like a pig, as well. The fucker still had his hat and sunglasses on, though his glasses were now a little bent.

Peck smiled. "They got the slip on us, amigo," he said, his words distorted by his mashed face.

"Callate!" a mean voice screamed from behind, stomping Peck on his lower back. Peck yelped in pain.

One of them was holding Peck's gun, so it was clear he'd already been searched. Now they fished around in all my pockets. One pulled out my cell phone, and I saw a piece of glass fall from the screen onto the ground. Another pulled a wad of cash from my pocket and stuffed it in his own. I could tell there were at least a handful of men working on us, though they seemed experienced enough to keep us from seeing them. I kept thinking, PLEASE don't put me in a fucking trunk again. PLEASE. They jerked us up to our feet and shoved us around, now limping and hopping. I saw a white van with the back doors open. The inside looked like a cage.

I finally got a brief look at some of our captors. They were tan with black hair, dressed in blue, short-sleeved shirts, kind of like plumbers, electricians, or any other utility worker. A man knocked Peck's hat back. It held on only by the chin-strap as they shoved a black bag over his head. Then a couple half-picked up Peck and slammed him into the back of the van. I could hear the bones in his face strike the metal like a bell. It hurt me to hear the noise. Now I knew it was my turn. In a flash, a black bag was over my head. I closed my eyes and tightened my facial muscles. It was all I could do as they hoisted me and slammed me inside, as well. Fortunately, my shoulder took the brunt of the force. The doors were quickly closed behind us, and we were in absolute, pitch-black darkness. In no time, I could feel the van rumbling away.

"Might be time to call out the cavalry," I spoke sarcastically into the darkness.

"Callate!" a voice suddenly screamed and hit me sharply in the head. Apparently Peck and I were not alone in the back of this van. I stayed quiet, and my mind raced with terrible thoughts of how horrible this was going to become.

6

El Brujo

We must have traveled for at least an hour. I could only re-breathe my own hot breath inside the filthy, cloth bag. The fabric against my face smelled like the old spit, sweat and fear of countless past victims, doomed in their own time just as I was now. My skull bounced up and down, banging painfully as we obviously tore around terrible roads. Aside from the crackles of earth below the tires, the only sounds were my and Peck's labored breathing. Though I knew one of our captors was inside the cargo section with us, he never made another sound.

There were eventually a few short stops, as if we were passing through checkpoints, and then we ascended sharply for a while. I was sliding back toward my feet. Finally, I felt the uneven ground shift into a smooth service, and I could hear men outside speaking in Spanish. There was a slight echo, like we were in a garage. Then I heard a great, metallic door rumble and slam down behind us. Soon afterward, the back of the van was opened, and I was yanked out by powerful hands and shoved around. I could barely walk, dizzy and disoriented, hardly able to breathe properly. I was helpless and numb. The bag stayed over my head, so the blackness persisted. After walking up and down a series of steps, and barely remaining upright a few times, I was finally forced down onto a hard, concrete floor. Then I heard a large door shut and lock. I had obviously been put into some kind of holding cell. They had left me bound and hoodwinked. It was so quiet I presumed I was alone.

"Peck," I called out. There was no response. "Peck." Again, nothing.

I rolled around and shimmied toward the wall, rubbing my head against the side of the cell, trying to swipe off the bag. I tried over and over again, but to no avail. For whatever reason, I simply couldn't get it off. Being left there, motionless and still in the quiet, burning up and confined, a stinging rush of panic finally swept over me. I felt like I couldn't breathe at all, and a powerful, insane urge gripped my body, involuntarily making me scream and flop around. I was simply and truly freaking the fuck out. However, it did absolutely no good. At some point, by the good grace of Jesus, I must have passed out.

Ultimately, under those kinds of conditions, time becomes meaningless. I can't say for sure how long as I was there, but I next recall the stifling pain in my arms and legs from being stuck in the same position such a long time. This awareness was triggered by the sound of the door opening. Under normal circumstances, I probably would never have even noticed the amount of fresh air that rushed inside. However, under these conditions, it was a wonderful feeling, like a cool fan had been turned on, and I could fill my lungs with precious life, even while still under the bag. Hands grabbed me and pulled me to my feet. This time, I actually couldn't stand up at first. I wobbled around, and they more or less dragged me.

They finally pushed me down into a chair. I sat there for a few minutes, breathing heavily. And then, in an instant, the bag was whipped off my head. Everything was blurry at first. I was in a large, dark room, and there were silhouettes of men darting about. I turned to my left. Peck was beside me. Hatless, Peck just had salt-and-pepper bristles of hair, and a trickle of blood had run down his right cheekbone. His glasses were gone. I'd never seen him look so helpless. The sardonic confidence I had always seen in his face was now gone. I turned back to get a better look at the room. It was frightening and beautiful at the same time.

There were a few windows in the distance, and I could see it was nighttime outside. I could tell the room was very large, but most of it was dark. In fact, it was kind of lit like the stage of an expensive theater, with certain elements highlighted, and the rest hidden away. An ominous metal pole stood in the center. The walls were greenish. But most surprisingly, everywhere I looked were lavish ritualistic decorations. Beads hung in various configurations, and colorful statues, made of finely carved wood, stone, or precious metals were highlighted on the walls. All of the art looked very "alien," reminding me of big-eyed exotic visitors, but it was clear much of this was Taino. I had always felt the Taino symbols looked otherworldly. Here and there, highly polished, intricately-decorated gourds hung from the ceiling. Some of them looked like ornate skulls. And strewn about either hanging on a wall, or from a corner, I saw weird bundles of things that looked like carefully-bound bones. There was an odd smell of eerily-pleasant incense burning. It was a lot to take in. And it was especially weird that Peck and I were basically unguarded. The dozen or so men in the room were carrying shadowy objects around, but no longer paying attention to us. They seemed to be preparing for something, and raw fear re-emerged at the forefront of my mind.

Suddenly, a motion caught my eye. It was an odd, dark, graceful form, almost like I'd caught a glimpse of a phantom in my peripheral vision. Usually, it's gone when you look at it directly. But not this time.

On the far side of the room, a man's tall, slender form entered. At first, I could only tell he wore a long robe. Just as I saw him, I could sense that he saw me too. Within moments, this figure almost seemed to glide out of the shadows. He moved toward us like a jaguar. Each step on the floor was as noiseless as a paw. When he stood before me, then leaned down to look me in the eye, I shuddered with a chill, despite the steamy air.

There was not a hair on his body, and his skin was black as night. His eyes glinted like yellow topaz gemstones.

His brown robe fell comfortably down his thin frame. He examined me pleasurably, as if he were a dragon, peering down into a hole in his cave, curious and amused by who had been small and foolish enough to tread there. And when he'd had his fill of me, his attention turned to Peck, marveling at him just the same. Peck scowled at him. Surely, this was El Brujo.

With almost supernatural ease, the figure rose, appearing very satisfied, then turned and walked back across the room. I looked at Peck.

"El Brujo?" I asked.

"Yes," Peck growled. "That's him."

When I returned my gaze to the space in front of us, I realized there was some kind of throne off in the shadows. It was wooden, covered in vine-like features, and El Brujo eased himself into it. He was primarily in darkness, but his face was nicely revealed by a soft shaft of orangish light from an angled lamp above.

A worker humbly walked up to El Brujo. The man was dressed in a dark-brown long-sleeved shirt and blue jeans, along with thick boots. He spoke respectfully in Spanish.

"Si," El Brujo said. His voice was deep and hollow.

The workman nodded, bowed his head, turned then walked away. He motioned to a few other men, and they quickly followed the workman off and out through a door behind El Brujo's throne. The rest of the men, apparently no longer needed, took various seats in the shadows. All became quiet and tense.

A few minutes later, the workman reappeared. He and his assistants were dragging a strangely-shaped object. I couldn't tell what it was at first. Once they re-entered the center light, my heart skipped a beat. They were dragging a man. He looked very Puerto Rican, perhaps in his 30s, wearing a polo shirt, nice pants, and leather shoes. His eyes were wild and crazed with fear. He was bound with a ball-gag shoved in his mouth. They pulled him over near the pole and stopped, looking over to El Brujo, as if awaiting instructions.

"Continuar," he motioned.

With precise coordination, the workmen unbound the man, leaving him gagged, and began removing his clothes; shoes first, then shirt, then socks, then pants. They were being surprisingly careful in the task, taking their time and making sure each item of fabric was removed and folded. Soon the man stood naked and trembling. He didn't resist at all, and they mechanically rebound his hands, this time to the pole in the middle of the stage. Oh God. I knew I was about to see something horrible. The only question was: how horrible?

The workmen now took their seats, and this poor man stood there, exposed, his arms locked back behind himself, around the pole. The room was still and silent for a while. I knew whatever was about to happen, it was partly a show for me and Peck. This was in line with the psychological trauma Peck had told me El Brujo enjoyed inflicting on his victims.

El Brujo closed his yellow eyes, and it seemed there was almost a period of meditation or prayer. And then, his eyes opened with a flash of madness.

He shouted, commanded, with force, "Vejigantes!" As soon as the words escaped his lips, a blood-curdling scene emerged.

A drum began to beat, and from the doorway behind him, a troop of six figures entered. Each figure wore a horrific, beastly mask. Apparently carved of wood, slightly-crooked, spiny projectiles radiated from each head like a crest of foot-long horns. Every mask was slightly different, but all were splashed with bright colors—red, white, green, blue, black and yellow—and speckled with tribal patterns. Their suits were long, colorful, flowing drape-like robes. Some opened their arms to reveal rippling wings of fabric, like the skin of flying squirrels, cascading from their wrists to their ankles. These were the traditional demons of Spanish lore, often celebrated in Ponce's annual carnaval, but there was no joy to be found in this room.

The vejigantes marched slowly toward the man like a death squad. That's when I realized two in the back were pounding the resonant drums. And two others in the rear shared the task of hauling a large, heavy cast iron cauldron and thick, black chains. For some reason, in this moment of unsettling terror, my mind recalled the disturbing, electronic soundtrack to Kubrick's A Clockwork Orange.

As the demons approached their victim, I noticed the two up front held small objects in their hands, obviously some instruments of torture. The man attached to the pole literally changed color. His once-tan face was now white, drained of blood. His eyes were filled with the panic I'd once seen in the eyes of a drowning man when I was a kid. I glanced over at Peck, and he at me. I don't think either of us really wanted to watch this. But I did.

The vejigantes at the lead, with long black horns and red faces, raised the objects in their hands. They were simple, metal pliers. I looked over at El Brujo. He relished the fact his face was in the light, and his expression was happy and content. I could easily see that he believed something wonderful was about to happen. Now noises were coming from the victim as he struggled, in vain, to speak. He was no doubt begging for his life, and surely offering up anything imaginable in return. But it didn't matter. We could all see what was happening was no bluff. If there had ever been a time for negotiation, it was long-past. No one batted an eye at his mournful sounds.

The vejigantes with pliers looked to El Brujo, and he nodded with approval. What happened next has haunted my sleep ever since. I am sorry to now implant this nightmare into your own psyche. But this is the truth of what I witnessed.

Quickly, and without hesitation, a vejigante clamped onto the man's nose and jerked it off in an instant. For a split-second, before blood gushed out, I saw his nose-less face in shock. Gagged, the victim howled in unimaginable agony as the other vejigante then used his pliers and ripped off the victim's left ear. Then off came the right. The victim squirmed and the most sickening noises came from him as the cold and emotionless vejigantes efficiently continued their work, jerking away chunks of flesh one plier-full at a time. Soon the man's lips were gone, then his nipples, then his penis, and the whole while the man seemed fully conscious of each and every brutal removal. I finally did look away. It was too much. I closed my eyes tight and gut wrenching thoughts entered my brain for the first time.

With the victim's gagged screams in the background, I remembered the first time I watched a video, on the internet, of an American being beheaded in the Middle East. I tried to put myself in that person's shoes, and I wondered what it must be like to finally confront the last moments of your violent death. We live our entire lives full of messages of hope and optimism. Whenever we're down on our luck, people encourage us and say we can get another chance, and how much they love us, and remind us that faith in Jesus is all that matters. No matter how bad things get, a part of us always believes, somewhere inside, no matter how small, that this will pass, and that goodness and justice will miraculously prevail. But what happens when all that hope, all those wishes, finally disappear? It occurs the instant the first irreplaceable flesh fails, or is blown away in war, or is ripped away by a killer. It is the most horrible feeling to suddenly shift from not knowing the future, to knowing it absolutely, and seeing that the future is utter pain. Then, the most you can hope for is the mercy of a short life, reducing that horrific pain until, God-willing, it actually does stop once you die.

You can imagine how relieved I was when the victim was finally quiet. Who knows at what part of the process he lost consciousness or died? Regardless, the vejigantes continued pulling pieces off of him for 30 minutes or so, until all that remained was a bloody skeleton hanging from the pole, right next to a big pile of bloody, dripping flesh oozing all over the floor.

"Bueno! Bueno!" El Brujo finally called.

Upon hearing this, the vejigantes quickly unbound the sagging skeleton, and the bones, still attached by rubbery ligaments, collapsed onto the floor. They then worked together to scoop up the skeleton and stuff it, little-by-little, into the cauldron. They used their pliers to snap bones when need be, and the crackling and breaking sounds were awful as they did their best to shove as much as possible into the evil metal bowl. El Brujo stood and walked over to the site, observing their work approvingly.

I was surprised they were actually able to fit the man's entire skeleton into the cauldron, but they did. And soon the vejigantes were working together, winding the long, thick, black chain around it, running it through the handle loops, and passing it over and over, from top to bottom, side to side, until the cauldron was almost hidden below a shell of links. They put several old padlocks on it, in various places, then set to work shoveling up the flesh and dumping it into a trash bag. Who knows where it would end up?

After supervising the work, El Brujo turned his yellow eyes to us. I squirmed. He began walking toward me, and just as before, his body seemed to glide, arriving sooner than it should have. He leaned down to my face once again, and raised a bony index finger with a long, well-polished fingernail. His eyes were filled with even more fire than before, and I couldn't help but recoil from him.

"Now," he said with a thick accent, "his soul belong to me."

Goosebumps erupted all over my flesh. I repressed a shudder running down my spine and did something very strange. I smiled and shook my head approvingly. And it wasn't a nervous smile. It was a survival instinct, yes-I-un-derstand-and-that-was-awesome smile. He seemed to like my reaction. El Brujo ignored Peck, stood, looked over to some of his men and flicked his wrist authoritatively.

In no time, bags were jammed back on our heads, and I was being dragged back into the holding cell. Before, the idea of being in that space had seemed like hell on earth. But now it was the most marvelous, wonderful gift I could ever imagine. I wanted to leap for joy back into that cell. And, better yet, before they tossed me back in, on the cold hard floor, they removed the hoodwink and unbound me. Though I thought I'd broken my wrist catching myself on the hard, cold concrete, I knew how lucky I was to be alive intact. They slammed the door behind me, and I rubbed out my sore joints in the darkness.

Now that I knew what El Brujo did to people, my mind raced with thoughts on how to get the fuck outta there or kill the men who opened the door and then get the fuck outta there. But first, I was growing very, very thirsty, and there wasn't a drop of water. The longer I sat alone in the darkness, the more thirsty I became. I dwelled on this for a long time. Finally, to cope with the feeling, I laid down on the unyielding floor and miserably went to sleep.

The boundary between the states of sleep and wake are blurred and awful when you are sealed in a lightless, isolated chamber. I don't know how often I was awake or asleep. It all seemed the same. The floor was bone-crunchingly hard. The only real gauge I had as to the passing of time was my thirst. At some point, I became hungry as hell, too, but the craving for liquid became unbearable. The discomfort of my body dissolved into the background as I began to fantasize about gulping down water. It didn't matter if it was nice and cold, or from a warm, filthy puddle. Dreams of drinking fluid ran over and over in my mind. I was fixated on it; obsessed. And I began to wonder if El Brujo's plan was to let us die of thirst. What a horrible death that would be. In fact, the more I thought about it, that would probably be even worse than being torn apart like the other guy. Imagine how it feels to slowly and simply dry up.

* * *

I was hallucinating by the time the door opened up again. I was lying on my back, devoid of energy. Strong hands jerked me out by the ankles and propped me up. I felt drunk as I was being dragged along, lights and hallways passing by. I was ready to die; anything to be out of this. I remember a lot of shapes and light and doorways. Eventually, I was thrown down on a dirt floor. I just laid there for a while. I didn't want to move. I just wanted to be still and die. I knew the dying process had already commenced within me.

"Here!" a voice called. I opened my eyes. I was lying at the bottom of a rectangular pit, and El Brujo stood at the edge above. He tossed down something heavy. It hit my stomach and I bolted upright. I felt like throwing up, but there was nothing inside me. Next to me was a plastic bottle of water. My hands trembled, and I fumbled to grab it and twist off the top. I was confused. Once it was open, I gulped it down, choking along the way. For a moment, I felt like throwing up from the water. I looked over to see Peck sitting right next to me. He was sipping his bottle.

"You gotta take it easy," he croaked. "Take it slow."

"Want more?" El Brujo called down from above. It looked like we were already in the grave.

"Yes! Please!" I shouted back up. I'm not sure how deep we were, but it was less than ten feet.

El Brujo tossed down a couple more bottles.

"Take it easy," Peck said again. "Slow amigo."

This time, I relaxed a little and just sipped it. My internal organs actually hurt as they awoke. I could feel my insides like never before as the cool liquid ran through.

Peck and I probably sat there for an hour, slowly pouring the water through our cracked lips. And I was actually starting to feel quite good. In fact, both of us were improving amazingly fast. We didn't speak to each other, but we definitely stared at each other with disgusted expressions. There was a lot to be disgusted about, so I'm not sure what we were both thinking at any given time. Finally, El Brujo appeared again at the top of the pit and loomed over us.

"Are you hungry?" he seemed to ask sincerely.

"Yes," Peck said.

"Yes, please," I said.

"Okay," El Brujo smiled. "This is all you get. So eat well!"

With that, El Brujo raised a bucket and quickly poured its contents down on us. I saw a thick, brown shower fall out, so I thought perhaps it would be dog food or something equally degrading. In fact, it was much worse than that. The moment the substance hit the floor of the pit, it was alive and squirming, racing in all directions.

"Centipedes!" Peck screamed, launching to his feet.

I fumbled backward hysterically and scrambled to my feet, as well.

These reddish-brown centipedes were incredibly long,

fat and healthy. At eight to twelve inches each, dozens of long, hooked legs scampered on each squiggly body. Some were actually darting for us, and around us, aggressively.

"Don't get bitten!" Peck shouted, jumping around. "They're poisonous!"

I could hear El Brujo laughing hysterically above.

"Careful! But jump on them!" Peck advised. He began quickly stomping out, then leaping back. Then stomping out and leaping back again.

Each time I jumped out and stomped, I could hear and feel a crunch under my shoes, but it wasn't accomplishing anything. They wouldn't just mash like worms. These creatures had a hard, outer armor that could withstand immense pressure.

"Don't stop!" Peck exclaimed, breathless. "Kill them all!"

I was wearing shorts, and one of them raced up my leg, its little limbs gripping into my flesh. It was a hair-raising sensation, and I was able to fling it off before it sunk its venomous mandibles into me. Peck and I just kept stomping and stomping, like lunatics. It was a hard workout, especially since we were barely able to walk. But after a while, they were all dead. Amazingly, neither one of us had sustained a bite. We were doubled over, heaving for breath. We would have been sweating, but there just wasn't enough water in our glands. Instead, we were overheating.

"Ha! Ha! Ha!" laughed El Brujo from above. "What a funny dance!"

Peck and I both collapsed back against the wall and tried to calm ourselves.

"But now you have a lot to eat!" El Brujo continued taunting us.

Peck looked up at him, and then he steadied himself on the wall of the pit and rose. Peck stared straight up at his captor for a bit, then he leaned over, reached out and pulled out a long, limp centipede.

"Thank you El Brujo," he said. Peck shoved most of it in his mouth and whipped his head to the side like a dog, ripping away the head. I could hear the hard crunching as he chomped and ground it in his jaws. "Delicioso!" Peck called up.

El Brujo stood and looked down for a while. He seemed a bit unsure of how to react. "You are very strong," he called down. "But you should keep eating. It is all you will have for a while."

Peck plopped down, grabbed another one, and began munching on it. I just sat there watching him. Occasionally, he spit out a leg. I couldn't remember the last time I ate, but I didn't feel hungry at all.

"You'd better eat them," Peck said. "Just don't eat their heads. Most of the poison is up there around their heads."

I looked over at the pile of dead centipedes in front of us. "I can't," I said.

"You need energy," Peck replied, pulling out another one.

"How are we gonna get outta here?" I whispered.

Suddenly the door to the pit slammed open. A group of Puerto Rico men stood there. They looked at us as I stared up with a blank face. They were obviously ready to take us back to our cells.

"Eat!" a guy with a mustache said. I turned away. The man leaned down next to me, picked up a centipede, put his hand on my shoulder, and wanted me to watch as he devoured one, same as Peck had been doing. It was a strange moment. I actually felt some measure of compassion was being shown toward us by this man.

"Not so bad," he said, and smiled.

His gesture actually meant something to me. Perhaps I was delirious enough to experience some measure of Stockholm Syndrome, but I was compelled to fish out a nice specimen and, in a rush, pushed it in my mouth, bite off the body and quickly chewed. There was a horrible sour taste under the stiff, brittle, and chewy shell. The legs were like little bones. But I just kept chewing and chewing and chewing. Finally, I swallowed the nasty thing. It felt good to have a little something solid in my belly.

"Okay," our guards said, urging us to rise. Once we stood up, black bags were thrown back over our heads, and I was stumbling, once again, through unfamiliar corridors. I ended up back inside the same cell, lying on the same concrete floor.

So what would be next? Would it be dying of thirst again? Or would I be sacrificed? Or would there be some kind of other creative and fucked up torture I would endure? All I knew was that I was in darkness again; in the world where time was just a vague sense. I would have never guessed what surreal scenario presented itself next.

*   *   *

The next time the door creaked open, I just kept laying there. I didn't even know what was real and what was not at first. Two men entered and eased me up onto my feet. I was wobbly again, but strangely enough, they seemed to take their time, caring for me a bit more. I felt less like a prisoner as they helped me walk out and up the stairs. I wasn't blindfolded, so I felt more like a human rather than an animal. We were in some narrow, drafty halls, and we went up and down a great many stairs, obviously leading to somewhere a good distance from the holding cell.

We finally emerged into a lavish area, like the living room of a nice jungle house. It had high ceilings, with split beam rafters. There was a bar, adorned with lit candles, and through large, open windows, I could see a nice view of the mountains outside. We passed across this room and through a large, outside doorway, onto an open deck. It was high up above the lush vegetation, mounted on posts, and a wooden rail closed off the sides. The sweeping view of steep, green mountains in all directions was breathtaking. The sun was low in the sky, and shadows on the ridges fell in striking creases of black against the craggy, jade-colored terrain.

A peaceful wind-chime sung in the breeze. A wicker dinner table was nicely set, and El Brujo sat at the far end. He stood when I entered. I was seated across from him. There was a space behind him with an expensive grill in place. A Puerto Rican cook, dressed in white, comfortable, puffy clothes, and a small white cap, was preparing it. The men who had guided me there walked off, and a few moments later, a couple other men emerged with Peck. He was wearing his hat and glasses again. They seated him to my left. I looked over at him. He had grayish stubble on his face, and a black eye. Someone had obviously popped him good in the face. Brujo nodded to Peck's captors, and they, too walked away. Now, here we were, Peck and I, unbound, sitting at a dinner table with El Brujo. The only other person was the cook, and he was busy about his work, paying us no mind.

El Brujo soared over us like a giant. He was relaxed, completely in control. He lifted a large, green bottle of Perrier sparkling water, cracked off the top, and poured a tall glass for each of us. Peck and I lifted our glasses and drank deeply. The bubbles were strong, and burned slightly on the way down. It was the best thing I had ever tasted. The water was quickly gone, and so El Brujo refilled our glasses, emptying the bottle. Again, we both gulped down the pure, refreshing liquid. Though our goal had been to kill him, he was now like a Bond villain, hosting us at his table. I felt this must be some ceremonial prerequisite to something awful. He was teasing us.

To stress his level of comfort, he actually turned his back to us and stepped over to the railing, gazing out on the healthy ranges sprawling before him.

"Look," he said, pointing. We turned our heads and saw white towers rising a short distance away, on the other side of a low peak. "That is the Arecibo dish," he said proudly, "the largest satellite dish in the world. It is a phone to the beings in cosmos, and it is mine."

"It's not yours," Peck defied him. Slightly incensed, El Brujo quickly defended his statement.

"Oh, it is mine," he snapped. "It is a beautiful thing that can sit quietly and listen to the softest whispers from space, harmonies from the past, light years away. Or I transmit 10,000 million watts through it and vaporize every creature in the sky. It is the biggest gun on the island, and I control this island."

"If you controlled this island, how did I kill all your scum so easily?" Peck retorted.

El Brujo sat back down across from us. "Yes," he said. "Thank you for taking care of that problem for me. They had all become too greedy. It was time for them to go. You saved me a lot of trouble. If I had wanted to, I could have stopped you at any moment. So many times I've had eyes on you, admiring you, and watching how stupid those men were. Their egos were so big, they were easy targets. On the island, we burn the brush to tame the wild weeds and fertilize the new growth. It was time for this for me. I am El Brujo. I know what is happening. I have learned to understand God."

"If you understood God, your mind would explode, dude," Peck said with disgust.

El Brujo laughed. "You two are hungry, yes?"

Peck and I just stared at him with bloodshot eyes, afraid to respond.

"Don't worry. You are the guests at my table tonight, so you will eat what I eat."

I glanced over to the grill, but there was no food visible.

"In fact," El Brujo said, "there is dinner, just now." He motioned behind me. I turned to find a large, fat, bright-green male iguana quietly creeping on the deck. He looked like a little dragon.

"Have you eaten iguana?" asked El Brujo.

"I have," said Peck.

"No," I said.

"Oh," El Brujo seemed to take interest in my response. "Then it is a tradition. You must be the one to kill it. Bring him to the grill, and I will give you a knife, and you can hack off his head."

I sat still, wondering what kind of little trick this must be. I looked at Peck. "I'll do it," Peck said.

"No," El Brujo responded firmly. "He must do it."

"Fine," I bolted confidently upright. I'd caught my share of snakes in Tennessee, so how much different could this be? I stood and moved toward the iguana. It froze. Then, in a hard, fast, precise motion, I struck, grabbing him by the throat and lifting him into the air. My grip was firm, and the iguana opened its mouth wide, scampering in the air with its long, ancient claws. A gooey string of spit clung from the top of its mouth to the bottom, hanging over a threatening row of tiny, razor-sharp, triangular teeth. I held it proudly, like a trophy, and looked El Brujo in the eye triumphantly. Then, much to my surprise, the iguana wrapped its long, spiny tail around my forearm and squeezed for a moment like a snake. Then, in one burst of force, jerked its tail back. The spines ripped through my arm like saw teeth.

"FUCK!" I shouted, and threw the iguana down on the deck. It landed with a heavy plop, and seemed stunned. El Brujo laughed heartily. The cook quickly ran over with a large kitchen knife and hacked off the lizard's head. It flopped around for a while, but I was more interested in the gash that spiraled around my arm.

"Good job!"El Brujo clapped his hands together once in glee. "That was a noble effort, young man. You dazed him for us. Ha! Ha! Ha!" He stood up. "Come inside my friends. We should wash that." El Brujo walked nonchalantly by, then held his hand toward the inside door.

"After you." Peck and I ambled past him and back into the living room-type area. He guided us over to the candle-lit bar. Behind it was a sink. I washed my cut profusely. It wasn't quite as deep as I'd originally thought, it was just bleeding quite a bit. I noticed that Peck was taking this opportunity to scan the inside of the room intently.

There were a number of intricate bottles around the room. El Brujo reached for some, opened it and asked to see my arm. I held out the wound, and he poured a dark-brown potion into it. It stung.

"What is that?" I asked.

"It's from the rainforest," he replied. "Smell it."

I raised my arm and sniffed it. It had a weird, medicinal odor, similar to an old cologne, but I couldn't place the aroma.

There was a bottle of white wine on the bar. "Would you care for some wine?" asked El Brujo.

"Sure, I'll have some," I said.

"No thank you," Peck replied. "I think I know this little game."

"And what game is that?" El Brujo tilted his head in curiosity as he pulled the cork from the wine and proceeded to pour me a glass.

"Have you ever eaten Kobe beef, Bill?" Peck asked me as he watched me lift the glass.

"No," I said, taking a sip. "What's that?"

"It comes from some very special cows in Japan," Peck said. "They're treated like kings. They get massaged every day, and fed beer and good food. They're in good spirits, and that way they taste even better when they're slaughtered."

"Do you imply that I intend to eat you for dinner?" asked El Brujo.

"Not a single cow on planet earth knows that people eat cows," Peck stated.

El Brujo chuckled, and reached to open a new bottle of white wine. "Do you know the author Robert Louis Stevenson?" he asked me. "Treasure Island? Dr. Jekyll and Mister Hyde?"

"Yeah," I said.

"Do you know how he died?" asked El Brujo, twising in the corkscrew.

"No," I replied.

"He was talking to his wife and straining to open a bottle of wine. Suddenly, he said 'Did you hear that?' Then he fell to the ground dead. Something had popped in his head." POP! The cork came out, and he reached over to carefully pour some fresh wine into my glass.

"Most men die on the toilet," Peck said flatly. "Think about that the next time you're squeezing one out."

El Brujo looked at Peck with condescension. "Especially if you are in the bathroom, senor." He held out his long arm, directing us back outside to the dinner table.

By the time we walked back onto the deck, the sun had almost set. There was a candle on our table now, and a plate of fresh fruit at each seat. In the background, I could see the cook skinning the iguana, peeling and rolling back its thick outer layers to reveal pink meat beneath. He paused once in a while to toss pieces on the grill. I could hear the sizzle, and I salivated at the delicious smoky, smells. We wasted no time cleaning the fruit from our plates.

"Look out over the treetops," El Brujo said. "Can you see the little heads of the iguanas?" I strained for a bit, but then, sure enough, I could make out the nearly-camouflaged forms of lizard heads poking up from leaves at the tree line.

"Ah yes, I see them," I said.

"Do you know they can predict the weather?"

"How?" I asked.

"When you get a good look at one on a branch, his body will tell you. If he is facing the trunk of the tree, rain is on the way. But if he is facing outward, it will remain clear. They are very in-tune with the rhythms of mother nature."

When the iguana meat was finally delivered, we devoured it madly. It tasted like the most tender, well-seasoned beef I had ever eaten. I was surprised. Then again, I had also been starving. None of us spoke during the meal. It didn't last very long, even though the cook provided a puffed pastry at the end before leaving to allow us private discussion. Having water, wine and food in my belly made me drowsy with joy. The experience had been very pleasant. In fact, the setting itself was almost romantic. We had eaten everything with our hands, and yet that large knife the cook had used was still there, next to the grill. I noticed Peck's eyes cutting over to it from time to time. So did El Brujo.

"You are a true killer, aren't you?" El Brujo said to Peck, retrieving a long, black cigar from somewhere and casually lighting it. A ring of smoke encircled his head, framing his hypnotic visage like that of a genuine wizard.

"So are you," said Peck.

"No, no, no," El Brujo took a deep drag and exhaled. "I am not like you. I only sacrifice when I need to take the spirits, and put them in a caldero, to be used. Most people just stay alive, down in my cells, until I need them."

"How come there are no guards here?" I asked.

El Brujo grinned, the candlelight flickering off his features. "Because you cannot hurt me."

"Are there cameras?" I asked.

"No, no, no," El Brujo seemed amused. "Many, many men have come here to kill me for many, many years. But they do not understand it is impossible."

"Why is that?" I asked.

"All around this island, there are empty graves. That is because I take the bodies from the graves and put them into my calderos, and bind them up with chains. And then I feed them with blood, with alcohol, with tobacco, with coffee. And their spirits reawaken, and are beholden to me. And when I take a fresh, living man, it is even more powerful. Every soul becomes my slave in the real world— the spirit world—and I reward them. Your weak, material eyes see no guards around me. And yet, if you had only a glimpse into the other world, like this," he snapped his fingers, "you would see the army of guards standing all around me."

Peck and I sat silent, and watched him enjoy his cigar.

"Stand up Bill," he said to me. Cautiously, I rose. "Take the knife," he instructed me flippantly. I was unsure of how to react. "No, go on. Really," he prodded. "Take it. I will not stop you."

I walked over and picked up the knife. It was long and sharp. Only a strong blade would have cut apart the iguana. I looked at El Brujo. He remained seated. "Now come here," he said.

"Come and put it to my throat." Again, I stood, my mind lost. "I will not hurt you," he continued. "I promise. Come. Do it."

Peck sat steady, his face unemotional. I walked over to El Brujo at the shadowy table and looked down at him. He stared up at me, his eyes shining like crystal facets. He calmly leaned back his head. "Go on." I gripped the knife and held it right under his chin. It felt as if the blade lightly touched his skin. "You can kill me," he said. "I will not stop you."

My heart pounded, and I could feel sweat on my palm. The dizziness was back. I turned, slammed the knife down on the table, and quickly took back my seat with great relief.

"You see," El Brujo smiled, taking another puff, "they will not let me be harmed. My magic is real."

I sat there breathing hard, uncertain of the feelings I had inside. Then I looked at El Brujo. He seemed very satisfied with himself.

"Let him try," I motioned to Peck. El Brujo and Peck instantly locked eyes. For a moment they seemed like two gunslingers at a poker table, each realizing a no-bullshit challenge had been thrown down. "If it's real, it will work on anyone, right?"

You could see the wheels turning in El Brujo's head, and for the first time, he looked slightly uncomfortable. The sounds of the nighttime creatures in the forest, along with the dangling wind chimes, magnified as we waited for his response.

"Okay," said El Brujo. "I will prove it. Give him the knife."

Peck's glasses were off. He slowly stood, and looked very carefully at El Brujo. Then he walked over, picked up the knife, and slashed El Brujo's throat. A horizontal line of blood sprayed from the deep gash. The wizard's eyes exploded into supernovas of horror, and desperate gurgles came from the hole. Peck dropped the knife back on the table, took off his hat, reached inside the lining, and pulled out a small object.

"I have the BALL of the Vampire of Moca!" he shouted in El Brujo's face. A plate and glass crashed to the floor as El Brujo collapsed, his hands futilely reaching and grasping. Soon he was quiet.

In the midst of this, I had bolted up and away from the bloodshed. Peck looked at me, still holding the testicle. "See amigo. It worked."

"We need to get the fuck out of here," I almost exclaimed, but quickly caught myself and lowered my voice. "What do we do?"

"We're gonna have to climb down these poles and head for the jungle, amigo"

"Okay," I said.

"But wait," Peck's confidence had fully returned. "I need to grab some things first. Wait right here and be quiet!"

He dashed back into the living room. I stood there in a panic. El Brujo was dead on the floor only feet away, and if his men discovered us, I couldn't imagine the chilling things that would likely happen. I grabbed the knife. I don't know what had prevented me from killing such an evil man myself. But now I knew I must kill to survive if we were found. There had been a good deal of noise, and it was entirely possible that someone had heard us. Come on Peck, I thought. Hurry the fuck up! Let's go!

When Peck finally came back, he was holding two objects. One of them was a flashlight. The other looked like a decorated gourd. He snatched his glasses and tossed me the flashlight.

"Don't turn this on yet, but we're gonna need it once we're in the weeds. This ain't gonna be easy, but take your time. You go first, amigo."

I walked over to the corner of the deck, and hoisted myself up and over the railing. Once I stood on the other side, I squatted down to feel the pole. It had a rough texture, which was good. "I'm just gonna try to shimmy down it," I said.

"Good. Go for it," Peck replied.

It was actually scary as hell trying to orient my body

properly and then make my way down this long drop in the darkness. Once I had let go of the railing, I was hugging the pole for dear life. I felt like a bear hanging onto a tree. I started working my way down, ignoring the occasional splinter. Even worse was the iguana cut on my arm. The wound kept being pulled open, then closed, over and over as I used every surface of my body to control the descent. The weakness from being in captivity so long also made a big difference. My usual strengths were long gone. But my mind, and willpower, was now stronger than ever. It probably took a long-ass five minutes before I finally felt brush touching my legs, and then the salvation of my feet on the soil.

I looked up and could barely see Peck's black silhouette.

"Here," he called down. "Catch this! And be careful with it."

He dropped the object he'd been carrying. It landed in my arms like a wooden football. Once Peck got close to the bottom, he just jumped down, landing like an oaf in the underbrush.

"Are you okay?" I asked.

"Yeah, yeah, I'm fine. Now, let's go."

"Do you know exactly where we are?"

"Not exactly," Peck replied. "But remember the big towers near the Arecibo dish? Let's just try to head in that direction. Once we get far enough away, we'll turn on the flashlight."

I handed him back the gourd. "Why did you take this?"

"I'll tell you later, amgio. You'll see."

7

That Which Never Changes

I opened my eyes. There was a slight coolness in the air. I was leaned up against the huge trunk of a tall tree, vegetation around me. At first, all seemed peaceful, then I jarred up, a streak of panic shooting through my blood. My head darted back and forth. Peck was asleep next to me, slumped up against the same tree. I didn't know where the hell I was. I forced myself to calm down and think. Still, my thoughts and memories were clouded. Calm down. Calm down. Where are you? Where are you?

My memory was gone. It just wasn't there. Then, all at once, my memory snapped back. It was like it had been floating far away in another dimension. Once my desire for it sent a cerebral signal, it kicked in and clicked back down the pipeline. The past few days of nightmarish captivity were all there, and I recalled that Peck and I had desperately hacked through roots, mud, water, stones, and sharp vines all night. Finally, our bodies were physically drained, and we had collapsed next to this tree. I had instantly fallen asleep—or whatever this state of mind could be called. Once the initial panic passed, the green-ery in front of me seemed like a protective blanket, and I just wanted to lie still. I felt like a child, imagining I could simply vanish, or teleport out of this situation. Only then was I aware of prickly bugs crawling on my flesh. I slapped them away, and shot up even straighter.

Peck was snoring. I wasn't sure whether or not I should awaken him, or simply let him sleep. But I felt so dehydrated and worried, that I nudged him.

"Peck," I said. He didn't wake up. "Peck." He was still out cold. I continued resting there, hearing the birds chirp all around me. Suddenly, they stopped. Behind me, I heard a loud hiss. I sprang to my feet, and saw a long snake wriggling on the tree right where I had been. It was tan with dark splotches. I couldn't help but jump up and down. "PECK!" I screamed.

"What amigo!" he angrily awoke.

"S . . . Snake! There's a fuckin' snake!"

He, too, was on his feet so quickly that I couldn't even see how he transitioned. "Oh crap," he rasped, gazing down at the thin boa. The decorated gourd was still on the ground, and the snake was creeping toward it. Peck leapt in to grab it, and the agitated snake struck like lightning. It missed him, and Peck tumbled backward into the brush. I helped him up, and pulled him to his feet as we continued backing away.

"They're not poisonous," Peck assured me. "They're okay." We tore off further through the jungle. When we finally plopped back down again, I watched Peck hugging the gourd.

"What the fuck is in there?" I asked, frustrated.

"He's in here," Peck said intently.

"Who?"

Peck lifted up the object, and I got the first good look at it. Indeed, it appeared to be a highly-shellacked and polished, dark-brown gourd. A royal row of beads and jewels looped around it like the adornment of a Faberge egg. "HE is, dude."

I calmed my heavy breath. "The alien?"

"Yes," Peck replied. "The most intelligent being in the universe."

"Is in there?"

"That's right, amigo."

I stared at Peck for a moment. "Let me see him."

"I will, but not right now."

"He's awfully small, isn't he?"

"That's a matter of opinion, amigo," Peck sounded slightly miffed. "Time and space are flexible to an advanced being."

"Well then why the fuck is he in there?"

"It's a safe place for now. But we're here to send him home, just like ET."

"And how are we gonna do that?"

"We've gotta go to the Arecibo dish. That's where it works best on this island. That's why it's there. And once he's home, my mission will be fulfilled, and so will yours, amigo."

"All right," I acquiesced, "I just wanna get the hell outta these woods. Now that it's daylight, what are we gonna do if El Brujo's men find us?"

"El Brujo is dead," Peck reminded me. "We don't have to worry about that motherfucker ever again. His men are probably already fighting each other over all his shit. They're stripping that place down and running away. They know that if El Brujo could be killed, they're totally screwed."

"Well then why don't you go ahead and call for backup finally and let's split? Can't they send a helicopter for us or something?"

"I will," Peck was becoming defensive. "I will when the mission is accomplished. That's how it works."

I stared wearily down at the ground.

"For now, we just keep walking till we hit water. Then we follow the water and it'll soon lead us to a house. There, we'll get our shit together. Okay?"

"All right," I stood up. "Let's go." We marched back into the growth.

Over the next couple hours of strenuous walking, up and down hills, the sky became darker and more gray. When it's about to rain in Puerto Rico, the black, menacing clouds start to roil and mound like the churning gates of hell are finally going to explode above. It is an unsettling feeling. One moment, there is not a drop in the air, and next moment, non-stop buckets of icy water are mercilessly drowning you. Because of this, narrow canyons with tiny streams can quickly become raging, deadly rapids. We had indeed been following a creek bed, but we knew we must soon head for higher ground. Right around then, we heard echoes of a dog barking somewhere ahead.

As we continued trudging between the banks of a tight ravine, we began to see more signs of civilization. Pieces of junk peeked out from the growth. There were tires and chunks of rusty metal. And finally, as the dog's barking increased, we saw a house up ahead, mounted above, in a good safe position atop the wet, leafy canyon we'd been traversing.

"I think we can get up here," Peck spotted a muddy little trail, most likely the path the dog, and other animals, would use to reach the creek for a sip. We carefully, slowly slipped and slid as we moved up the path, grabbing onto flimsy weeds for support. Soon we saw the dog, a medium-sized white and brown mutt, with a tinge of hound. Despite his barking, his tail wagged, and he looked friendly. The shabby little house he guarded appeared isolated, completely surrounded by woods. However, there was an old, beat up truck in front, and I thought I could hear a radio playing inside.

When we topped the bank, the pooch ran over and started sniffing us. I petted him. He was especially interested in Peck and the object he carried. We looked up to see a man standing next to the house. This was the moment of truth. What kind of reception would we get? He was short, wearing a ragged, light-blue baseball cap, dirty t-shirt, faded blue jeans, and muddy boots. He had a little black mustache. For some reason, with his combination of dress and posture, he almost blended in with the background. The house, the surrounding forest, and him, all shared the same washed out colors and tones.

"Hola!" Peck threw up his hand.

"Buena!" the man replied in a thin, thickly-accented voice, with a brief wave.

A huge, cold drop of water landed on my head with a plop and a splash. A whooshing sound zoomed up, and the rain exploded over us. It seemed no more discussion was warranted. We all ran like hell for the house, including the dog. There was a partially propped-up covered porch, and it felt, and sounded, like it might break to pieces when we all pounced on it. You'd have thought Mount Vesuvius was erupting overhead. The water on the roof was deafening, and his yard (if you could call it that) had turned into a flowing, muddy sheet of water. Mists were spraying in at all sides, and he quickly ushered us into his small house with laughter.

"You saved us amigo!" Peck exclaimed as the man slammed the door behind us and the hound pounded around our feet goofily. The man laughed and looked downward.

"Ahh . . ." he said. "Mi . . . My English is not so good."

"You sound good to me, amigo!" Peck said, removing his glasses and wiping them off. "Thank you for having us in. Muchas gracias amigo."

"You very welcome," replied the man. He extended his hand. "I am Julio. I was born in July."

Peck chuckled and took his hand. "My name is Richard," they shook.

"And I'm Bill," I shook, as well.

"Okay," said Julio. "And this is Pablo," he pointed down to the dog. Pablo raised up with excitement, wagging his tail furiously as Julio petted him.

"Hola Pablo," said Peck, bending down to pet him briskly, as well.

"Are you hiking?" Julio inquired.

"Oh my God, amigo," Peck replied dramatically. "You wouldn't believe what we've been through." Julio furrowed his brow.

"I am a photographer," Peck said. "I work for National Geographic. And Bill, my assistant, and I have been working in the woods trying to capture photos of the elusive monkeys, but they robbed us."

"De monkeys?" Julio raised his brow.

"Yes," Peck said.

Oh fuck, I thought to myself.

"Well actually," Peck stammered a bit, "first it was the monkeys and then it was men. Bandidos."

"Oh no," said Julio. "There are some bad men in deese woods."

"Yeah, no kidding, amigo," Peck shook his head.

"Well come, please, and sit down," Julio showed us to a broken-down couch in his tiny living room. I was amazed to see a huge, flat-screen, high-definition television. Julio turned it on and we were watching ESPN in vivid, blazing glory.

"Wow," I said, "this is a nice TV."

"Yes, thank you," Julio replied, as he was scurrying off to a little dark hallway. "How you say? I had to . . . eat a lot of pussy for that."

Julio vanished and Peck and I looked at each other blankly. "Well, that was kind of inappropriate," Peck said.

Everything took on a weirder tone from that point. Peck and I sat still watching this glorious television with the smelly, wet canine between us. In a few moments, Julio returned with two towels and handed them to us.

"Oh, muchas gracias," I said. We wiped off the moisture. The towel felt warm so, I was happy to just pull it around myself like a security blanket when I was done.

"You need something to drink or eat?" asked Julio.

"Yes!" we both said.

"I don't have a lot, but I can make ham and cheese sandwich."

"YES!" we both exclaimed again. My mouth watered at the mere thought of it. I was ravenously hungry again.

"And some water, please," Peck begged. "Lots and lots of water."

Julio rushed us over a couple of tall plastics cups of

tap water. It was slightly brown, but we gulped it down anyway.

"Need more?" asked Julio.

"Yes please," Peck said, and we both held out our cups. Julio returned with more water, and then milled around in the fridge. He slapped together a paper plate of some basic sandwiches—just white bread with slices of ham and cheese—and Peck and I scarfed them down like animals.

"You guys were really hungry!" Julio said, sitting in crappy little folding chair next to us.

"Yes," Peck leaned back and sighed with relief. "You have no idea how much we thank you, amigo."

"What is that?" asked Julio, pointing to the gourd.

"This," Peck said, "is a . . . prop. It's a piece of art, and I was supposed to shoot it with the monkeys." Julio seemed confused. "Yeah, it's just some artsy-fartsy shit. You know."

"Oh, okay," Julio said. "So should I call the policia?"

"No, no, no," Peck stressed. "I'm insured by my employer, and we'll get all this worked out privately."

"Okay," Julio sounded a bit skeptical.

"What do you do for a living, amigo?" Peck asked.

"I am a . . . how you say . . . technician. I work on the observatorio."

"Really?" Peck perked up. "And what do you do?"

"I climb up towers and make adjustment."

"That is absolutely fascinating," Peck said. "So you have access to the big dish?"

"Si, I mean yes," Julio responded.

"And how did you get that job?" Peck inquired.

"Oh, I was born here, and I am not afraid of heights," he laughed hysterically and we joined in courteously.

"Well you have a very nice place here," Peck said. "Do you live here alone?"

"I do now," he said. Pablo hopped into his lap and he stroked him lovingly. "I was married, but she is gone now."

"Oh," Peck said. "Well I'm sorry to hear that."

"Yeah," said Pablo. "We were together for 20 years, but she was not a nice lady. She beat me down. Wore me down. Like when you pound on metal, a little by a little, a year by a year. You keep wearing away again and again and finally that was me." He laughed hysterically again.

"Oh, okay," Peck laughed along.

"So is good that she is gone. And now I have the TV!" Julio couldn't stop laughing now.

This guy was definitely a strange bird. But then again, we seemed to be in the right company.

"Where are you from?" Julio inquired.

"I'm from North Carolina," Peck replied.

"And I'm from Tennessee," I said.

"Oh okay. My brother was in North Carolina in the military," Julio said. "Would you like more food?"

"Well," Peck responded hesitantly. "Maybe. How about you Bill?"

"Yes," I said, "I could eat more."

"Okay," Julio stood up. The rain had passed, and now we could only hear a peaceful drizzle outside. "I need to get cigarrillos. I will go buy some more stuff to eat and drink."

"Oh, that would be wonderful," Peck rolled back his head. "I will pay you back, amigo, I promise."

"Is okay, is okay," said Julio. "You relax and I will be back soon." He walked out the door and his truck sounded rickety as he pulled away.

Peck and I sat on the couch, the dog now curled up and sleeping next to me.

"Nice guy, huh?" said Peck.

"Yep," I said. "Seems to be."

*　*　*

The front door banged open, and I jarred up. I had fallen asleep on the couch, and so had Peck. The warm pooch had been totally peaceful between us, but he too, bolted up when I did. Peck was still sleeping like a baby, almost leaning off the side of the couch, cuddling with the gourd. I turned to see Julio, holding two bags, struggling to make it back inside and set them on the counter. The bags were unstable, and he was delicately pulling out various items and placing them down on the hard surface. I got up and raced over to help him.

"Gracia," he said.

There were numerous bottles of beer, apples, bread, cheese, meats, milk, and potato chips. "I just got a few things," he said.

"Oh my God, this looks amazing," I replied.

"Now let me tell you something about this refrigerator," Julio explained as he opened the door. "It gets cold in different places. If you put meat or something like that in this bottom, right-hand drawer, it doesn't get cold enough. So that stuff goes in the left-hand drawer. And if you put stuff on this middle rack, it gets good and cold like it should. But if you put something on this top rack, in the right-hand corner, it will freeze. So that is bad for meat and beer . . ."

Thirty minutes later, we were all sitting in the living room watching a ballgame and pigging out. Just as we were all crunching the last chips, Peck asked Julio about the dish.

"So part of my assignment was to take pictures of the dish," Peck lied. "How long have you worked on it?"

"Since I was a kid," Julio nodded. "My papa did all the work cutting the bushes, and I used to help him. So I worked around the observatorio my whole life."

"I need to get very close to it," Peck said.

"There is a museum there," Julio responded, "and you can look right down on the whole thing."

"No, I need to get closer than that. I need to get right on the edge of it," Peck sounded very serious.

"You have to be careful if you are not used to it," Julio placed his plate down on the flimsy, old table in front of us. "It will . . . play tricks with your mind." He lifted an index finger and swirled it around his left temple.

"What kind of tricks?" Peck asked.

"Oh," Julio looked into the air as if searching for the right answer. "It is like it talks to you sometimes, inside your brain. You know harp?"

"HAARP?" Peck perked up. "H-A-A-R-P?" he spelled it out.

"Si, si. Yes. H-A-A-R-P."

"Oh I know HAARP all right," Peck shook his head.

"What is HAARP?" I asked.

"The High Frequency Active Auroral Research Project," Peck sounded proud that he could remember it all. "It was an operation started by the Air Force, Navy, University of Alaska and DARPA. They have a giant grid of antennas in Alaska transmitting massive radio broadcasts onto tiny little sections of the ionosphere. They can short circuit the earth's electric field to create a giant lightning bolt and destroy cities. Or they can tune it back to just control weather, or tune it back even more and make subtle little waves that fuck with people's minds. And the project has expanded with transmitting antennas all over Puerto Rico, centered around Arecibo."

"Yes, yes," Julio was nodding, his eyes closed, and pointing his index finger, backing up Peck's words all the way.

"So what have you been experiencing?" Peck asked.

"Ahh, well . . ." Julio's eyes were searching for how to explain it. "Basically, voices talking to me."

"Voices?" Peck prodded him along.

"Si. Si. They are voices in my mind."

"What do they say?" Peck asked.

"Well," Julio thought deeply in order to answer accurately, "it depends. Different things. Sometimes it is just random words. But other times it is a message, the same message, over and over again."

"Yes," Peck leaned forward. "What is the message?"

"Well," Julio continued. "It is a voice that says: 'Do not be afraid. Something big is about to happen on this island, but you will be okay.'"

You could have heard a pin drop. "Did you hear that Bill?" Peck turned to me. "Does that sound familiar, amigo?"

I contemplated it all for a minute. It was eerie to hear Julio say the same words that Peck had said to me about the ball of light. I spoke up. "What's so special about this island?"

"I told you amigo," Peck emphasized his words, "the gravity is low, and this is where the first land appeared around here millions of years ago. It's the first alien base."

"Yeah, but what do you think?" I asked Julio. "Why here?"

He thought for a moment. "I tell you what," he said. "I have lived here my entire life, and lots of old men have lived and died and said they saw these things when they were little kids. And there are lots of thoughts on this. But the truth is . . . the real truth is that nobody knows."

We were all quiet for a bit, then Peck said, "So what kind of access is there to the dish?"

"Oh," Julio slightly lifted his hands and bobbed his head about, "there is the museum that opens at . . ."

"No I mean tonight," Peck interjected.

"Oh," Julio seemed surprised. "Tonight there is nothing."

"But you said you have access, right?"

"Oh yes, senor, I have access to a short tower right beside the dish when maintenance tests needs to be done, but it is not for the general public."

"Well we need to go there tonight," Peck said.

Julio looked confused. He shifted his head from Peck to me, and then back to Peck again.

"Why?"

"It's a long story," Peck said. Oh great, I thought, that's a fucking good one.

"But," Julio looked helpless, "I can't just go on the towers without authorization."

"Do you have keys?" asked Peck.

"Well," Julio hesitated, "yes, I have keys. But I need authorization to use them."

"I am an agent of the United States government," Peck announced, "and I am giving you authorization to use them tonight."

"You mean . . . National Geographic?" Julio seemed discombobulated.

"You're goddamn right," Peck responded forcefully. "But not just that. I also work for the CIA, NSA, FBI, and a bunch of other shit you don't even know exists. Comprehende?"

Julio just sat there and looked at him blankly for a while.

"Entiendo?" Peck asked.

"Si," Julio replied, though it sounded more like a question than an affirmation. "But I need to have a form 403."

"We don't need a Form 403," Peck shot back.

"But, yes," Julio said. "We always need a Form 403."

"All right," Peck said, rising from his seat and handing me the gourd. He walked a few feet over to the kitchen area, pulled out a drawer, and removed a long, serrated knife.

"Peck," I called to him. He ignored me, and walked over to Julio. Pablo started barking.

"Peck!" I said, standing up.

Peck held the knife up to Julio's throat.

"Peck, what the fuck are you doing!" I shouted. "This man saved us. He's been nice to us. What the fuck are you doing?"

"Did you know El Brujo's dead, Julio?" Peck spoke lowly. Julio's eyes were filled with terror. "He had a little throat problem, too. Didn't he Bill?"

"Yes," I said. I looked Julio in the eye. "Yes he did."

"And Julio," Peck shook his head. "If you will not give me your access to the tower, next to the dish, you're gonna have a throat problem, too. Do you understand, amigo?"

Julio sadly shot his eyes up to Peck, and then over to me. He could see that I was helpless, and Peck was in complete control.

"Si," he said. "I understand."

"So," Peck dictated, like a terrorist, "we're gonna get in your truck and go to the tower and you're gonna give us access to the dish. Si?"

"Si."

"And you understand that if you fuck around, you will die. Si?"

"Si."

I was disgusted to see Peck as such a bully. I wanted to believe he would not actually cut Julio's throat, but I knew he might. As far as I knew, this was a totally innocent man who had simply helped us. Maybe Peck knew something about him that I did not, but it still sickened me to see Peck treat him this way. As Julio grabbed the truck keys and headed outside with a knife pointed at him, Peck looked to me and said "Whatever it takes, amigo. Whatever it takes."

Peck grabbed the gourd and flashlight, and the three of us walked into the muggy night, over the creaking porch, and across the grass to Julio's old truck. Julio got behind the wheel, Peck squooshed next to him with the knife, and I was in the passenger seat. I had to slam the door hard a couple times since it set askew in its frame. "Remember amigo," Peck said softly to Julio, "you just get us there, and no harm will come to you."

"Okay," Julio nodded.

He cranked up the old beast and we were soon bumping up and down on terrible, gravel roads, barely penetrating the dense vegetation hanging all around. Despite the fact this twisted experience with Dick Peck was not over, I still felt incredibly relieved, as if I had done my part, and now I was literally along for the ride. I kept reaching for my pocket to pull out my cell phone, and then remembering it was gone.

Little by little, other shabby little houses appeared in the headlights. Most of them seemed rather dreary, and some had roofs crammed with piles of small satellite dishes. "Why do all these houses have dishes, too?" I asked.

"These are people, just regular people, who are also in contact here with the voices." Julio explained. "So they make their own stations at home to listen."

"Weird," I said, still unsure of what to think about this whole thing.

Signs began to appear on these rough roads, somewhat guiding the way to the dish. They were ragged, and written in Spanish, so it was clear these were for the employees and not the public. We finally encountered a rather basic gate, sealed only with a padlock and chain. We stopped and waited while Julio got out, opened it, then pulled the truck on through and closed it again behind us. We did this a couple more times with similar gates. There was never another soul around, yet the closer we got to the dish, the more glimpses we had of guide wires, large metal boxes, transformers, and similar technical infrastructure.

"Boy, this would be a good damn time for an abduction, wouldn't it?" said Peck.

"Yeah, I guess so," I replied.

"This is perfect," Peck's looked all around, marveling, his imagination firing. "We're in this old, shitty truck at night, out in the middle of the jungle driving toward the Arecibo satellite, and all of a sudden, we round a curve and a big-ass fucking UFO is just sitting there, blowing smoke and steam, waiting to zip us off into outer space like Close Encounters of the Third Kind. Man, if that's ever gonna happen, this is the absolute perfect fucking time. Can you see that?"

"Yes," I said. "I can see that happening."

"How about you, Julio?" Peck asked. "Have you ever seen any crazy shit like that out here?"

"Uh, I have seen weird lights in the sky," Julio said. "But nothing in de road. One time I saw a big white light over top of de dish. It just sat there like a planet or a big, bright star. I was with two other guys, and we got on de radio and asked everybody what we were seeing. No one had an explanation. Then, all of a sudden, de white light changed. It looked like two wings popped out on both sides of it, and then red, blue and green lights started to swirl and blink around. And we were standing there trying to figure out what we were seeing. And all of a sudden, it just shot away into de sky in de blink of an eye. We all sat up all de rest of the night talking about it over and over and over again."

"What about missing time?" asked Peck.

"I'm sorry?" Julio squinted.

"Missing time," Peck reiterated. "Like when one minute you're fine and the next minute you've jumped hours ahead, like you can't remember what happened over the past few hours."

"Let me explain something that most people don't realize," Peck said. "When a guy is in a truck, on a desolated road, and there is suddenly a UFO overhead, the truck stops working. Then the guy is sitting there helpless, in the dark, looking up at a mother ship. Then the UFO flies off and instantly the guy's truck starts working again. He doesn't have to turn the ignition again. The damn thing just starts working. Do you realize what that means?"

Julio and I were both silent, not exactly sure of what he was talking about.

"Think about it!" Peck seemed agitated. "What the fuck do you think that means?"

"What?" I said.

"It means that they're not just disrupting the mechanics of the vehicle. They're stopping time, amigo. Their craft is producing a wave of energy that is changing gravity, space and time. And that one thing, manipulating time, is what all these paranormal phenomena have in common. When somebody sees a ghost, what are they doing? They're looking back in time. When somebody is on the trail of bigfoot, or the chupacabra, and he vanishes in mid-trail, he has obviously changed his point in space. And since time and space are connected, he has not only changed his relationship to space, but also his relationship to time. It's time! Time! Time! That's the key amigos. And that's why you shouldn't obsess over it."

Peck was sounding more and more like a rambling maniac, but I played along. I nodded my head as if he'd just spoken the most profound words I'd ever heard. Julio did the same.

"And furthermore, do you know there are statistics to determine when you have the best chances of being abducted?" continued Peck. "According to reams of data that has been archived by the United States government, you have the highest possible chances of being taken away by extraterrestrial or inter-dimensional beings on a Wednesday night, after 10pm, driving somewhere in Arizona or New Mexico, in a blue four-door car, if you are a male school teacher over the age of forty and your first name is Fred. Now how fucked up is THAT?"

Finally, in the distance, a truly awe-inspiring sight emerged. Up ahead, I could see what, at first, looked like one massive edge of a gigantic, shining, flying saucer on the forest floor. I had only seen photos of the dish from above. I had no idea that when one was directly beside it, the wall rose so high. Julio finally stopped the truck next to a white tower right at the edge of the dish. When we hopped out, I felt like an ant staring up at a mammoth bowl.

Even though Julio had been there a million times, I

sensed that even he stared up at the dish with reverence and awe. Peck was silent. For the first time, he looked almost like he was standing in a cathedral. He finally took a deep breath and looked at me. "Can you feel it amigo?"

"Yeah," I said. "I think so."

"Time flows differently here," Peck meditated. Then he turned his attention to Julio. "Doesn't it?" he honestly inquired.

"Yes," said Julio. "Sometimes faster, sometimes slower, but always different."

"That's why they built it right here," Peck kept staring up. "This is the portal."

"What's it made out of?" I asked.

"Almost 40 thousand aluminum panels," Julio answered. "They are perfectly aligned to create one big dish. I'm a little guy, so sometimes I get to walk out onto the dish to do repairs. It's bigger than three football fields from side to side. And if they started to transmit while I was out there, I would have burst into one big fireball!"

"That's amazing," I marveled.

"So what do you want here?" Julio scratched his sweaty brow beneath the rim of his hat. "You don't have a camera with you."

"I don't need a camera," Peck replied. "I have something different to do. You see, amigo," Peck spoke to him kindly, "I can hear the voices, too."

"Oh?" Julio perked up.

"But they say something different to me," Peck

explained. "At first, when I came here, and started hearing voices, I thought I might be going crazy. But then I heard about the other people on the island who could also hear voices, and I realized what was happening here. This is the island that connects us to the other side. Some of us are very in-tune with it, but there is a slightly different message for everyone."

"Okay," Julio seemed to easily accept Peck's words.

"So here's what I need you to do for me, amigo," Peck continued. "I want you to wait right down here with this truck. Bill and I are gonna climb up this tower by ourselves. When we come back down, I'm gonna have you drive us somewhere, and there I'm gonna pay you one thoushand dollars cash for your cooperation, and being a good, patriotic American. How does that sound?"

"But I am a Puerto Rican," Julio said.

"You're an American goddamnit," Peck said. "Red, white and blue, with Washington, Jefferson, Franklin and the U.S. Constitution flying over your ass. Hell, you're better than an American. You don't have to pay fucking taxes."

"Okay," said Julio. "One thousand dollars?"

"That's right," Peck reassured him.

"Okay," said Julio. "I can use that. I will be right here."

"Gracias amigo," Peck said warmly, and looked to me. "Let's go."

Julio unlocked a flimsy gate at the bottom of the thin tower. It swung open with a brittle creak, and Peck, gourd and flashlight in hand, led the way. It was a bit scary to walk onto the old, metal structure, as it seemed to bounce with each and every step. The higher we went up the narrow walkway, the more the whole thing swayed.

With each step, more and more of the dish was revealed in the pale, blue moonlight. The metal panels below were excellent reflectors of the light, and the higher we got, the more the dish looked like a lit crater on the moon, surrounded by darkness. Its size was yawning and powerful, haunting and beautiful in the night. When we finally reached the tiny, grated metal deck at the top, we were looking down at the very edge of the entire dish. It was an overwhelming, dream-like sight, and yet so close, I felt I could almost reach out and touch it. Peck and I sat down. Once motionless, we could especially feel the movement of the tall, flimsy structure. The two of us sat there in silent. It was a truly holy moment. For Peck, I felt this was the ideal marriage of science, spirituality, conspiracy and mysticism.

"Quite a sight, isn't it?" Peck said breathlessly.

"Yeah," I agreed. "I've never seen anything like it."

"It's our telephone to the great beyond," Peck stared down, then relaxed more, closing his eyes. "It's the place that ties it all together. Do you realize what we've done?"

"What?" I said, feeling drowsy from gazing at the majesty before me.

"We came here and won. We killed all these greedy bastards with our own two hands—just like I was told to do. And now we're gonna make the universe a better place. I'm gonna have Julio drive us to a nice hotel. We'll get some food and a good night's sleep. Then tomorrow I have a friend with a plane who will fly us back to the states, and we're gonna get your life sorted out and back on track. Okay, amigo?"

"Okay," I said.

"It's been a wild ride, amigo!" Peck grinned, his voice growling with delight. "Give me a hug!" Peck grabbed me and squeezed me lovingly in his arms. I hugged him back for a moment. Then Peck reclined again for a moment before holding up the sacred gourd. He stretched out his arm and held it before us, its shape eclipsing part of the dish. This was a juxtaposition that clearly meant a lot to him. He was sitting with his legs crossed Indian-style, and he tucked the gourd against his groin. I heard him take a deep breath. "I'm . . . I'm not sure I can do this," he sounded emotional. "Maybe . . . maybe you should do it."

"Do what?"

"Release him. Release our little friend and return the universe to its balance. Bring peace to all mankind and all our brothers across the vast light years of the sprawling, infinite space around us."

"All right," I said. "I'll do it. Let me see it."

Peck slowly, hesitantly, reached down and pulled up the gourd. Then he seemed to struggle, holding it out toward me. "Take it," he said.

I pulled the smooth, ebony form from his hands.

"Okay, never mind!" he jerked it back. "I'll do it, amigo. I must do it."

"All right, all right," I replied, "but we need to do this fast and get this over with. Julio is waiting."

"Yeah," Peck took another deep breath. "Here we go." He twisted the cap off the gourd and it came off like a lid. Slowly, slowly, he reached inside with his right hand. All expression had melted from his face, and the entirety of his mind and body was fixed on whatever delicate thing he would remove from within. I've only seen men deactivate bombs in the movies, and on television, but I can't imagine they would take more care than what I observed in Peck for that minute. Slowly, gently, he withdrew his hand and immediately cupped the other on top of it. He brought it toward his face, cracked his fingers and peered inside. He gasped and smiled with wonder, staring into his hands for the longest time. When he finally lowered his hand, he looked to me proudly. "Would you like to see him now?"

"Of course," I was impatient. "Let me see him!"

"Okay," Peck said, holding out his hands. He cracked his fingers open again and I held down my face. There was only darkness inside.

"Give me the flashlight," I said.

"Why?"

"Because I can't see him. I need the flashlight."

"You can't see him!?" Peck exclaimed, laughing with disbelief.

I pulled the flashlight out of Peck's left pocket and

turned it on. I peered inside Peck's hands. There, staring up at me, was a tiny coqui frog. It was no bigger than my pinky fingernail, tan-colored, with big, glossy black eyes. I shot my eyes up to Peck. "A frog?"

"A FROG!?" Peck laughed maniacally. "A frog? That's how he looks to you? Ha! Ha! Ha!"

"Yes," I replied. "A coqui."

Peck continued laughing. "That's rich," he chuckled. "He looks like a frog to you."

"What does he look like to you?" I asked, confused.

"He looks like . . ." Peck paused, "he looks like a marble of blinding divine light."

For some reason, I started to feel angry inside. "What do you mean. It's a frog," I said.

Peck pulled his hands close, holding the precious contents up against his breast. "Obviously, he can appear however he wants," Peck said matter-of-factly. "He is a master of manipulating matter. I think it's hilarious that the most intelligent being in the universe wants you to see him as a coqui."

This whole situation was now so ridiculous that it was beginning to offend me. I began to think that all the trauma had finally gotten to Peck and robbed his logic. He was hungry, thirsty, and tired. Surely he was hallucinating. And a chilling reality ran over me: if he had lost it, then it was now solely my responsibility to get us out of this mess and back to civilization to sort things out. "Okay," I said, "then let's go on and release him."

"Yes. You're right amigo." Peck looked sad. "Now is the time."

Peck held out his hands over the rail. The edge of the dish was a few feet below. "Go on A-O. You may return."

"A-O?" I said.

"Yes. That's what I call him," Peck closed his eyes confidently. "Alpha-Omega."

"Um hum," I voiced skeptically.

"Go on," Peck nudged him. "You can go back now."

In an instant, the coqui sprang, amazingly, from Peck's hands. His tiny, dark form sailed, in a beautiful arc, a surprising distance, through the evening air. It was almost like slow-motion. And then the frog, despite his ever-so-tiny weight, landed with a sticky plop on the surface of an instrument sensitive enough to capture invisible filaments of fine energy from the innermost expanses of deep space . . . and all hell broke loose.

Blinding spotlights turned on all around the dish, and a siren rang out in the air. The panels below us now shined as bright as the sun.

"Fuck!" I shouted, and Peck scrambled to his feet. Dazed by the sudden light, we banged around into the rails, practically climbing on top of each other, shoving our way back down the steps. The tower moaned and shifted violently from side-to-side as we raced down, skipping steps and tripping along the way.

When we finally reached the bottom, bright flashlights turned on, broken by the silhouettes of men holding rifles pointing toward us. "Freeze! FBI!" a man's powerful voice shouted. We both stopped dead in our tracks, raising our hands. Instantly, powerful grips were upon us, throwing us hard to the ground. A sharp knee clamped down on my neck, and a gun barrel was pressed to my head. The air was filled with Spanish shouts. We just laid there in the chaos, the taste of dirt in my mouth. There was more enthusiastic chattering. Then I could hear Julio's voice.

"That's the one!" he said. "That is the man who held us hostage!"

"This one?" a silhouette pointed toward me.

"No, no!" Julio exclaimed. "The other one. The one with the hat!" I heard Peck grunt, and the sound of him being whipped up. Shortly thereafter, I was pulled to my feet with a measure of respect. Julio hugged me. "Amigo," he said, "are you okay?"

"Uh . . . yeah . . . yes!" I said.

I looked over to see a crowd of dark figures with flashlights pulling Peck away into the darkness. Soon, a helicopter pounded the air ahead, beaming down a roving spotlight. I was utterly confused. I looked over at Julio, and he smiled at me.

Someone's hands brushed the dirt off my shoulder. I turned to see a tall man, wearing a dark suit, straightening up my shirt. "I'm very sorry sir," he said. "Are you okay?"

"Yes," I said.

"Good, good," the man replied courteously. "Stay right here. You're okay now. We got him. Okay?"

"Yeah, yeah," I nodded. The man had crew-cut hair, a square jaw, and tiny fucking ears. He turned and spoke into a radio, running off into the direction they had taken Peck. Julio and I were left alone. Julio relaxed on the hood of his truck. I stared at him.

"You're welcome, amigo," he said. "Your friend was loco. He was gonna kill me. And now you owe me."

"Yeah," I nodded. Then I reflected for a moment. "What do I owe you?" I asked.

"Your friend was going to pay me one thousand dollars. Now I want you to pay me five thousand dollars. This is very fair."

I dropped my head. I couldn't believe I had now just transitioned from one asshole to another. "This is bullshit," I said.

"Huh?" Julio couldn't believe I had said that.

"This whole thing is bullshit."

"Do you want to go to jail, amigo?" Julio said. "You need to chill de fuck out."

I stood there looking at him for a moment. Then I stared off at the oblivion where Peck had been dragged. I couldn't see what was happening, but I could hear lots of men talking and the sharp static of handheld radios cutting on and off amidst excited conversations. My logical mind seemed shot. And yet I looked in the direction of Peck, then back to Julio, then toward Peck over and over again, my mind racing. And finally, I felt I knew what to do.

In one smooth motion, I recoiled and popped Julio hard in the nose. He fell backward onto his truck with a thump, then rolled off the side and hit the ground hard. With that, I ran furiously into whatever growth was straight ahead. There could have been a damn cliff there, but I didn't care. I was now blinded with fury, electrified with a new surge of energy. Though they were there, I had no awareness of obstacles. Jagged branches, vines, and stones surely ripped at me, and poked my face. But I fled like a rabbit. My only direction was straight ahead, and the earth would conform to my path.

Everything was a blur of darkness. I could have slammed into a tree, knocking myself out, at any time. But I did not. For hours, I simply dashed, faster and faster, until my wobbly legs literally gave out, and I launched forward, crashing face-first into the leafy ground. Only then was I apparently unconscious.

✳ ✳ ✳

The next I can remember, the sun was up and I trudged, like a zombie, through the woods. My pockets were empty, and my stomach was full of sickness and fear. I finally stumbled upon a roadway. I had nowhere to go. I had never felt so directionless and alone in my entire life. I stood there, in the gray mist of morning, and held out my thumb to passing cars. I was surprised when one finally slowed down. It was a small, silver sedan. The door opened and a little old man named Kiko was inside. I plopped in, grateful, looking like dirty hell.

I'd never met a sweeter soul. I know my eyes were bleary, and grime was stuck to my sweaty skin, but he was only interested in helping me. I told him I was a tourist who had been hiking, and that I'd gotten lost and was robbed.

"I am so sorry," he said, embarrassed for his island. I wish I could have told him the truth, that everyone in Puerto Rico had always been very kind to me until I teamed up with another insane gringo and started delving into the drug world. But I could barely communicate articulately, and I had never before been in such need of mercy and charity. He started talking to me about Jesus, and I told him that I was a born-again Christian.

Kiko drove me to an ancient church in a dirty little town riddled with vagabonds. I climbed up the steps and was met by a small woman with curly brown hair and sad eyes. She took me to a weather-worn priest in a cramped back office. Neither of them spoke a lick of English, but Kiko talked to them. After some hesitation, they agreed to help me. In a little back kitchen, they gave me a warm bowl of soup, a chunk of stale bread, and a pitcher of Cool-Aid. When I was done, they showed me to a room in the basement with a hard cot. I collapsed onto it, and I think I slept for two days solid. When I finally woke up, and ambled up the stairs, the woman with sad eyes showed me to a shower. I wanted a hot shower, but all the water was cold.

Nevertheless, I stayed in there for a good hour. It was like a baptism, and when I emerged, I vowed my life was going to be different from now on.

My clothes were so dirty that the lady gave me an old, long-sleeved shirt and pants from a charity bin. And just before I left, she handed me sixty dollars and said "Kiko." Apparently, he had left that for me. I swear, when I saw those three twenty dollar bills, I felt like I had hit the lottery. I almost wanted to cry. It was amazing to go from having absolutely nothing, to having a caring person get me back on my feet. I would make that money go a long, damn way. But when I walked out the door, and found myself on the edge of a plaza, I realized I honestly did not know which way to turn, or what to do.

It was breezy, sunny peaceful day. Old men sat around playing dominos. Pigeons fumbled about here and there, and an occasional car drifted by with the windows down. It was like the volume of my life had gone from max to min, and I wasn't sure how to handle the transition. As I meandered around the plaza, one old guy came up and asked me if he could wash my windows. "I don't have a car," I said. He couldn't understand me. He kept trying to get money, and I just wanted to get away. I turned, and the first group of friendly faces I saw was on the sidewalk outside a weird little bar. It was more of a garage really, with the door open. There was a clear case full of fried meat-filled pastries, what they call empanadillas, on the western side of the island. I bolted into the bar and sat down. I was the only gringo.

The bartender looked about 15 years old. "Buenas," he said.

"Uh . . . una Medalla por favor," I replied.

"Okay," he pulled out a golden can, thumped it to make sure it wasn't frozen, cracked it open with a spew of mist and set it on the bar. "One fifty," he said.

I gave him a twenty. When I got my change, I let him keep two dollars. "Shit," I thought. "I'm already down to fifty-eight bucks." And then I realized that's how it starts. This may very well be day one in the wasted life of a drunken bum. Five years later, I could be slumped on the corner in San Juan, jingling a paper cup full of coins, my head hanging in misery, presenting the horrific, oozing, infected wound on my leg, living through hell on earth. No. Fuck that. I had to find out what had happened to Peck. But where could I start?

"Cheers," an accented voice said next to me.

To my left sat an unkempt, scruffy Puerto Rican guy in a worn t-shirt. He was holding up his Medalla to toast. "Cheers," I said, and we bumped cans. I turned up the Medalla and took a good, long swig of the cold, light beer.

"I start every day like this," the guy said. He sounded surprisingly articulate. "I pour a nice, cold Medalla into a chilled glass on the rocks. Once half-full, I shake in a few squirts of dark brown Angostura bitters, then fill it the rest of the way. Next I take a used pincho stick and stir it all into a frothy, amber frenzy. After it sits a minute or two, and the foam weakens, I down it in a string of impatient gulps, like the elixir of life itself. Sixty seconds after I'm done, the weight and worries of morning fade away magically. Nectar of the Gods."

I was amazed by his way with words. "You should be a writer," I said.

"I am," he replied. "And a bartender. I just come here to chill out and read the newspaper."

I glanced over at the paper in front of him. HOLY FUCKING SHIT. There was a big mug shot of Peck on the front page with a giant headline in Spanish. He looked terrible.

"What, what does that say?" I asked anxiously.

He casually lifted it up. "It says Drug Kingpin Nabbed."

"Would you mind reading me that?" I asked.

"The whole thing?"

"Just . . . Just start reading please."

The guy looked at me a little funny, then said "okay." And here's what he read . . .

San Juan – Just after 9pm Thursday night, FBI Agents, following a tip, arrested Juan Daniel Marcos, considered the largest drug trafficker in Puerto Rico. He was captured near the Arecibo Observatory after a killing spree to overthrow his competition on the island. One of the world's most wanted men, he was known to many as "Mr. Numbers," due to his neurotic need to keep detailed accounting and lists of his enemies and activities, a characteristic that is now helping law enforcement officials in their investigation. Though born on a military base in Puerto Rico, his parents moved to Tennessee when he was three years old. He was considered especially dangerous since he served three terms as the Sheriff of Sullivan County, Tennessee in the 1970s, before joining the DEA, and eventually being discharged in 1992 due to mental instability.

"Marcos used his background in law enforcement to access private records, manipulate people and outmaneuver us for years," Captain Paul McDivitt of the FBI said in a press conference.

Officials believe at least 50 murders, of both officers and suspected drug dealers, may be attributed to Marcos, including recent ones in San Juan, Ponce, and Cabo Rojo. Upon search of his residence in Tennessee, FBI agents found an incriminating list of people he planned to kill on his latest spree. All of them are now dead except the last name on the list. The FBI task force is trying to locate that individual for questioning.

When I first came to Puerto Rico, almost a year before all this, I had a nice little wad of cash in my pocket. I hitchhiked to a beach on the west coast called Playa Sucia. I'd never seen sand so powder-white, and water so radiant blue. As I rested on the beach, I felt like I was sitting in the middle of a Corona beer commercial. Later that day, I hopped a ride to another nearby beach called Combate. There, I rented a Jet Ski for a couple hours. It was the best two hours of my life. I revved it up full throttle, and blazed across the ocean at 55 miles per hour. The ocean was rough that day, and I leapt into the air, over and over again. Each time I slammed back down, the heavy machine under me would wobble and slide from side to side, like it was going to flip and throw me into the water. It was more frightening than fun, but I tamed it. I kept it under control, and blasted as far out into the ocean as I could. Finally, I stopped and turned off the engine. There I was, far, far out, all alone on the water. There was no sign of land or humankind as far as my eye could see in all directions. I bobbed up and down. At that moment, I realized that, ultimately, I was all alone in the world. I felt oddly enough, at complete peace.

And then, just as my mind wandered, I was startled to see the form of a giant fish glide by me, it's back just below the surface. I don't know exactly what kind of creature it was. But as soon as I saw it, my heart skipped a beat, and I remembered just how deep the ocean was there. Thousands and thousands of feet sprawled below me, filled with entire mountain ranges and worlds of life with no idea that humans also live in the world. And when I realized this, I was suddenly scared again. I felt as if I was floating vulnerably in the sky. I was like the cartoon character that begins to fall only when he realizes he is off the cliff. I quickly started the Jet Ski back up, and hauled ass toward the shore again. The loneliness scared me.

When I neared the jagged rocky shore, in the distance

was an old, gray lighthouse atop striking cliffs. It was a bold, amazing sight, and I slowly throttled by. The water was so clear that I could see every pebble on the sea floor, and each little fish darting about, or each jellyfish pulsating through like an alien. I later heard that a climactic moment in the movie Papillon, with Steve McQueen, had been shot there in the early 70s. The cliffs were over 200 feet high, a straight, unguarded drop into the ocean. It was a perfect place for suicide.

After dwelling on the article in the bar about Peck, I hitchhiked a ride with a couple from New York named Peter and Denise. They were tourists exploring the island, and I told them I was just a beach bum on vacation. We got along very well, especially since they were in a happy vacation mood. Time and time again, I thought about asking to use their cell to call my mom and sister, and maybe even my old girlfriend Christy. But I just couldn't make that call. Peter and Denise were on their way to Playa Sucia, and dropped me off with a free beer at the foot of the large hill where the Cabo Rojo lighthouse, what the locals call "el faro," is located.

We were all waving and smiling as they drove away. Then I turned and faced the solitary hike up the trail to the top of the cliffs. The walk was rocky, and the dry ground was covered with sharp and thistly brush. All was still and quiet. Though it was a nice day, I only passed a couple other people coming back down on my way up. When I reached the top, the stately lighthouse set to my left, empty and unguarded, where it had saved lives since 1882. But as I walked past it, and crested the hill, a great wind suddenly arose, pressing my shirt and pants against me like a blanket. With each step toward the edge of the cliff, the majestic sound of the waves below pounding against the rocks increased in volume.

Finally, when I reached the edge, I looked down at a breath-taking sight. The emerald-tinged aquamarine water was blinding and clear. The cliff was a long protrusion, like a mammoth serrated blade, running down the side of the hill. Before me, various towers of prehistoric rock, shaped like the spines of dinosaurs, jutted up from the huge, white waves crashing against them. Over eons of time, the water had worn holes into the stone, and when a particularly large wave swelled in the ocean then hit the harsh shore, a blowhole of salty spray would shoot high into the air.

When I looked down on this overwhelming scene, I was almost overcome by a pleasant dizziness. It was the sort of feeling that most people fear when standing near a straight, deadly drop of this kind. But on this day, under those circumstances, it was exactly what I wanted. It felt good. One piece of the cliff jutted out a good ways over the chasm below. I was overtaken by a pleasant numbness, and so I stepped out on the perch of stone and looked down. The tips of my tennis shoes were literally over the edge. As I stood there, staring down, it felt like there was an odd pulsation in the rock, coming up through my feet. The pulse increased into a surging throbbing, stronger and stronger. I wondered if this was simply my own blood pressure increasing while my entire body had entered this super-sensitive state. Maybe that's all it was, my awareness of my own body rising and falling against this extreme point of earth with each heartbeat. I could have simply closed my eyes and fallen into the wind. But instead, I sat down on the edge, dangling my feet over the side, absolutely fearless and foolish. I thought about closing my eyes and leaping into the wind.

I looked out over the water and thought about my life. I thought about the horizon I could see, and the sun beaming down, rippling in a mirrored stream across the ever-changing waves. I thought about everything that had led me to this point in my life. All my decisions, and all the things I had allowed myself to believe. And I wondered, deep inside, where was this man I knew called Peck? What had truly happened to him? Life is mad, yet there are some people who seem to make sense of it all. Whether or not they're right or wrong, when they're gone, it feels like we're back at square one.

The men who had gotten Peck would eventually get me, too. I was sure of it. I faced the reality: there would be no pardon for me. And yet, I looked deep inside, and I believed something. I believed that no matter what had happened, I could change everything now. I could turn

myself in, pay my dues, go home somehow to see my family and friends again, and be forgiven. I was not the first
person to fuck up, and if I went to Cabo Rojo and admitted my flaws, humbled myself and gave up, maybe then I
could begin rebuilding.

I thought about the Peck I knew, and the things he
said. And then I dwelled on the newspaper article over
and over again. I thought back in detail about our experiences, and what had actually occurred. I thought back on
all the fantastic things he'd told me about. But actually, I
had never seen any of it. Not one alien. Not one ghost. Not
one chupacabra. Not one bit of real magic. I hadn't seen
one thing that defied the laws of physics or revealed other
realms that somehow explain all the troubling and surreal
scenarios that leave us all confused and disturbed each
day, surely out of the loop somehow. Despite the vivid,
colorful images his conspiracies had created in my mind,
I had actually seen nothing.

Suddenly, something caught my eye in the distant
water ahead. It was a small sparkle, like a mirror had been
flicked, shining the sunlight toward me. It twinkled a few
times, and then it seemed to skip around, back and forth,
on the water for a while. What was this? Could it be a fish?
Some sort of bird? Some optical illusion this time of day?
It almost looked like a silvery little ball, dancing around
just at the surface. And then it was gone. I'd heard about
people staring out over these waters, at this very spot, just
like I was, shocked to see a giant USO suddenly launch

up from below, water running down and spewing from it, before it shot away at light speed. Oh Jesus, did I want to see that. Oh God, did I begin to believe.

Peck told me the Zen master said that what is real is that which never changes. Those days I spent with Peck, and all the things he told me, are forever locked into my mind. He said nothing is real. But now I know that he was wrong. Now I understand. I choose to believe. Now I know that everything—and I mean everything—is real.

Made in the USA
Middletown, DE
23 December 2024

68116820R00141